HAPPILY
EVER AFTER

•

Janet Avery

AVALON BOOKS
NEW YORK

PRINTED IN THE UNITED STATES OF AMERICA
ON ACID-FREE PAPER
BY HADDON CRAFTSMEN, BLOOMSBURG, PENNSYLVANIA

For Dominique, Randy, Jennifer, Melanie, and Heather with love and thanks. And for Gabby, the inspiration for "Horatio."

Chapter One

Quinn O'Connell stood on tiptoe, dusting a shelf and moving books to make room for a new self-help title that had come in that day. *The Spinster's Dilemma.* Quinn grimaced as she placed it spine-out next to one of her favorites, *Righteous Woman.* Honestly, what self-respecting, independent Nineties woman would even pick up a book with a title like that, never mind read it? The word spinster conjured up visions of gray-haired, bespectacled women of a certain age— women who looked a lot like the author of the book, she thought as she flipped it over to examine the cover photo.

Just because a woman wanted to make her own choices, was that reason to slap a label on her and call her unmarried state a problem? Quinn thought of her apartment and the peace she had, knowing if she wanted to paint the kitchen orange or put up a Picasso

1

print, no one was going to question her decision or complain about the cost. Men were just a lot of extra work anyway.

"Dani, do you think I'm a spinster?" Quinn called out in a rare moment of self-doubt to her coworker and friend who was unpacking another box of books in a far corner of the store.

"What in heaven's name has got into you?" Dani asked, her expression puzzled. "You're anything but old-fashioned and you're only thirty-five, for heaven's sake. Women our age are considered in their prime, not spinsters! We're attractive, independent career women." Dani's dark eyes flashed in defiance and, hands on her ample hips, she challenged anyone who dared to call her or Quinn that dreadful name. She thought for a moment, then added, "Does this have anything to do with your mother's constant attempts at matchmaking? Really, Quinn, I've told you before not to worry about her antics. She just wants you to be happy and, for her, that means marriage and parenthood. It was good enough for her, so why not you?"

Quinn stopped what she was doing and considered Dani's words.

"There's nothing wrong with marriage for those who want it, but I can look after myself, thank you very much. Who wants to be dependent on anyone, especially a man? They're so unpredictable!" she joked. "Besides, I've never met any man who can hold my attention long enough to get me thinking about marriage. And I absolutely refuse to take over from someone's mother—cooking and cleaning, moving to the suburbs, and having babies." Quinn looked disgusted at the thought of leaving the city and changing her free and easy lifestyle.

"You needn't worry; you can't cook worth a darn anyway. I've eaten at Chez O'Connell on more than one occasion, so I know from personal experience just how lacking you are in culinary skills," Dani teased.

Quinn relied heavily on packages of instant pasta and the frozen food section of the local supermarket for nourishment.

"I could never take up cooking as a serious pastime," Quinn insisted as if to defend her choice of lifestyle. "And as for housework, I vowed the moment I was making enough money, I'd hire one of those cleaning companies that come in once a week and shovel out the mess, and that's exactly what I've done. Nope, married life isn't for me," Quinn insisted emphatically. "Spinster or no, I like being a career woman."

Quinn looked around the bookstore she'd purchased three years before. Words Unlimited, her pride and joy, catered to women's interests, stocking everything from feminist writing to romance novels. Even books like *The Spinster's Dilemma* found a place on its shelves.

"I don't know about being attractive though, Dani. Do you think I am?" Quinn asked doubtfully. She wasn't fishing for compliments; she'd just never considered the possibility. She walked a few paces to the "staff only" section of the store and regarded herself in the full-length mirror, tacked on the back of the door. Reflected back at her was a tall, lanky woman with short, straight chestnut-colored hair that shone red in sunlight. The eyes returning her forthright gaze

were soft velvet brown, belying a look of steely determination. As always, she was dressed in jeans and
a sweatshirt, more interested in comfort than style, and
her casual clothes effectively hid a shapely figure.

"It's not because you're unattractive or boring that
you're not married, Quinn O'Connell. You could have
any man you wanted," Dani offered, a devilish look
crossing her face, "if only you weren't so ornery." She
laughed and ducked as Quinn threw her duster at her.

"Never mind, Dani." Quinn shrugged her shoulders
and went back to shelving books. "There isn't any man
I want. The only male in my life, other than Dad, is
Horatio, and I aim to keep it that way." Horatio, an
Old English sheepdog and Quinn's constant companion, was stretched out in the corner, his head resting
on his front paws. His ears perked when he heard his
name and he got up and ambled over to Quinn. He
was big and shaggy, his gray-and-white coat magnif-
icent, especially when Quinn brushed it, which she
loved to do. He slept in a corner at the store by day
and at the foot of Quinn's bed by night, guarding her
from unwelcome intruders. When she was ready to
welcome a man into her sanctuary he would have to
make friends with Horatio first. "Dad and Horatio
spoil me rotten and set an impossibly high standard, a
hard act for any mortal man to follow." Quinn
laughed.

"Speaking of Mother, though, that woman sure
knows how to get me riled, Dani. She invites me to
dinner and conveniently forgets to say she's invited
her friend, Hazel's son, or Aunt Teresa's nephew from
the other side of the family. 'You'll like him, Quinn,
he's a pediatrician,' " she mimicked her mother. "I'm

afraid to visit my parents for fear she'll play match-maker again."

The last time her mother had pulled this stunt had been a complete disaster. Quinn had driven all the way to Duncan after a busy Saturday at the store because her mother had asked her to dinner and wouldn't take no for an answer. Their conversation should have tipped Quinn off, but when her mother's call had come, she'd had a store full of customers, and had agreed absentmindedly to drive the thirty miles north to Duncan.

Later, as she locked the bookstore and opened the car door for Horatio, she replayed the conversation in her mind, and red lights had started flashing. The evening had been like so many others, an unmitigated disaster, with her mother's latest choice for son-in-law sitting awkwardly in the living room when she arrived, gaps in the conversation big enough to drive a truck through, and her mother's disappointment to deal with once it became clear that her latest attempt at match-making had failed.

The phone rang, and Quinn left it to Dani, who picked it up, then handed it to her.

"Speak of the devil," she whispered, smiling imp-ishly.

"Quinn, it's your mother. Remember me? You haven't called in weeks."

There she goes, trying to make me feel guilty, thought Quinn. "That's not true, Mother. I called the other day, but you were out playing bingo or canasta or something. I asked Dad to tell you I'd called," Quinn said, scarcely concealing her impatience.

"He must have forgotten. I could kill that man sometimes."

You will if you don't quit nagging him, Quinn thought to herself. Never would she dare to say such a thing out loud.

"Anyway, you've got me now, but there are people lined up at the counter here, so we'll have to be brief," Quinn said, crossing her fingers as she told her mother a little white lie. There was only one customer, and Dani was looking after her and didn't need help from Quinn.

"I want you here for dinner tonight." No polite request, her mother's invitation was a royal command.

"Not tonight, Mother," Quinn started, trying in vain to come up with an excuse quickly.

"Quinn, please," her mother insisted. "Your father's been feeling poorly lately. He was just saying this morning how he'd like to see you. Don't let him down. Besides, I'm cooking your favorite meal," she added slyly. "Lasagna, Caesar salad, and fresh homemade bread. And I've got an apple pie for dessert."

Her mother was up to something. She had the heavy artillery out. She knew Quinn had a soft spot for her father and would do anything for him. To top it off, she was offering a home-cooked meal, one which would lend itself to being packaged up as leftovers and brought home for dinners for the next few nights.

Quinn had been worried about her father of late. He'd had a heart attack the previous year and, although he'd made a good recovery, he tired easily. He wasn't getting any younger; soon he would celebrate his seventieth birthday.

"Okay, I'll come," she gave in gracefully, "but I can't be there before seven-thirty."

"That's perfect," her mother cooed. "And Quinn, change into a nice dress before you come." With that, Quinn had heard a click and the phone went dead.

That last remark of her mother's should have alerted Quinn that she was up to her old tricks, but Quinn got embroiled in hunting for a book for a customer and put the conversation out of her mind. It was the kind of day that kept her busy right up to closing time, and she was practically on her way to Duncan before she remembered her mother's words.

Of course, she had not changed out of the faded jeans and baggy sweater she'd worn to work. Once again she would run the risk of disappointing her mother. Quinn had made a habit of this. Not on purpose, of course—it was just that nothing she ever did was ever quite good enough to satisfy her mother's unreachable standards.

The scenery on the Malahat Highway, the stretch of road from Victoria to Duncan, was breathtaking at any time but even more so in the soft evening light. Shafts of sunlight pushed through the tall cedars, casting shadows in the mossy forest, and the red-barked arbutus trees stood out like beacons. Occasionally Quinn caught a glimpse of the numerous small islands grouped offshore: they were purple and green and floating on a calm, gray sea. She began to relax and unwind from her hectic day as she sped along.

The time passed quickly, and before she knew it she was on the outskirts of Duncan heading toward her parents' house. As she pulled into the driveway of their rancher on the city's outer limits, Quinn wondered whom her mother had mustered for inspection this time. Was there a new doctor in town, or was it her parents' accountant? Her mother had been mentioning him lately. She favored professional men, and worked tirelessly to interest Quinn, who invariably found them stuffy and humorless. There was no greater sin, in Quinn's book, than a man with no sense of humor.

Quinn gritted her teeth as she opened the car door for Horatio, trying in vain to keep him from trampling her mother's garden. It was mid-May and flowers were blooming profusely in hanging baskets, planters, and raised beds. Color ran riot. The garden had no particular theme; Marjorie O'Connell had tried to cover all the bases. As Quinn breathed in deeply and smelled the fragrant mixed perfume of the blossoms, she admitted her mother had done a terrific job. Aside from the confusion and clutter, the garden had a certain cachet with its jumble of pots and plants.

All at once it dawned on Quinn that Horatio was nowhere to be seen. While she'd been admiring the flowers, he had disappeared. As she looked around, trying to spot him, she heard a loud crash. A deep male voice swore profusely, then a dog yelped. Horatio came bursting through the hedge, followed closely by an angry man with a shovel raised over his head.

"What the heck—?" she started to say before being interrupted.

"Does this sorry excuse for a dog belong to you?" the irate man barked at her.

"Yes he does, and you can put that shovel down right now. What do you think you're doing? He didn't mean any harm. If he's broken something, I'll gladly pay for it."

Quinn stuck out her chin and folded her arms over her chest, challenging the stranger. Her face began to redden, as it always did when she got angry. The nerve of him, threatening Horatio!

"You bet you will. If you can't control your dog, you shouldn't be allowed to own one," the man growled, slowly lowering the shovel.

"Of all the miserable . . ." she tried again, but the stranger turned abruptly and stalked away, his back stiff and unbending. Quinn was left standing with her mouth agape.

Quinn hated confrontation. Normally she would do just about anything to avoid an argument. But Horatio was her baby, and she would never let anyone hurt him, not even if she had to do battle on his behalf. Not that she could be sure that horrible man had been planning to hit him with the shovel, but it had looked suspicious.

While Quinn was rushing to his defense, Horatio crouched behind the shelter of her long legs, belly on the ground, letting out an occasional whimper. For a ninety-pound dog he was such a big chicken.

"It's all right, Horatio, no one's going to hit you, not while I'm here." She bent to pat him, and he leaned into her hand and licked it gratefully. Of all the nerve! Quinn fumed.

She recalled her parents mentioning that the house next door had been sold but she hadn't realized the Walters, the elderly couple who had lived there, had already moved. They had always kept a supply of Horatio's favorite treats, and he had been accustomed to

calling on them whenever he and Quinn came to visit
her parents. It was natural that he would head over
there as soon as he jumped out of the car.

The Walters were moving to a retirement home.
That obnoxious, overbearing man must be their replacement. Too bad! Oh, well, the new neighbor was
her parents' problem, not hers. As long as she kept
Horatio where he belonged, on the right side of the
hedge, she wouldn't have to have anything to do with
him.

"Let's go, Horatio. We'll get you a treat."

The dog jumped up and ran to the side door of the
O'Connell home. Quinn's mother had a thing about
dogs, especially Horatio. He was only permitted in the
kitchen and didn't have free reign of the house as he
did at home. Oh, well, he'd be comfortable there, and
she could slip him a dog biscuit from time to time.
She rang the bell and walked in.

"Quinn, finally!" her mother greeted her. "We
thought you weren't going to make it." Looking Quinn
over, she frowned. "You didn't change. And what's
that smudge on your nose? Go wash up, dinner will
be ready shortly."

"Hello to you too, Mother." She kissed her mother's
cheek, smiling wryly as she rubbed at her nose. Why
was this tiny dynamo of a woman capable of reducing
her to age twelve with a few well-chosen words?

"Of course, hello." Marjorie pecked Quinn quickly
on the cheek and turned back to the stove where steam
rose from a madly boiling pot.

Impeccably dressed as usual, Marjorie O'Connell
looked younger than her sixty-eight years. Her graying
hair was combed in soft curls around her face. She'd

powdered her nose and applied a touch of pale pink
lipstick. She looked elegant, even down to the lacy
apron covering the front of her dress. Not that Quinn
was surprised. Her mother always looked smart. When
Quinn had been going through her gangly, awkward
teens, she'd felt totally inadequate next to her.

Quinn took after her father's side of the family. She
was five foot ten and slim. Next to her mother, who
was not much more than five feet, she felt like the
Friendly Giant and about as graceful. Perhaps that was
why she never wore the suits and dresses her mother
insisted on buying her. She could never look as elegant
as her mother and felt like a fraud when she tried.

Quinn settled Horatio in the kitchen and went
through the door into the living room to greet her father, who was sitting by the fireplace in his easy chair.
This was how she always pictured him when she was
back home at her apartment in Victoria and missing
him. At the sound of the door, he looked up from his
newspaper and got up to give her a hug. He was taller
than she by a couple of inches but slightly stooped, so
they appeared about the same height.

"What have you been up to, Dad? You look worn
out."

"Just a little gardening. I'm fine. Really," Howard
O'Connell insisted when he saw how worried she was.
"You look great."

"No I don't, you old softy, but thanks for saying so.
I can use the boost. Tell me, what's Mother got up her
sleeve tonight?"

"Don't be upset with her." He smiled. "She doesn't
mean any harm. It's just that we're not getting any
younger, and she'd like to live long enough to hold a

grandchild or two on her knee." He chuckled. "And so would I for that matter!"

Quinn felt a stab of fear shoot through her as she studied him. Was there something he wasn't telling her? She frowned unconsciously, running her hand through her hair.

"I'm fine, silly." He smiled and ruffled her hair. No one but her father could get away with that. Quinn hugged him again.

"Well, you and Mother would do better putting pressure on Carol and Jeff. I have no intention of getting married and I certainly don't want kids." Carol, her younger sister, had married Jeff Fraser a couple of years earlier.

"You'll change your tune, Quinn, when you meet the right man. You fuss over Horatio and treat *him* just like a baby. You've got lots of love in you. You don't want to become a dried-up old prune, do you?"

"Give me a break." Quinn laughed at his description. "You're beginning to sound just like Mother."

"That's what happens when you've been married as long as we have." He chuckled sheepishly. "You start to think and act with one voice."

"That's what I'm trying to avoid," Quinn joked.

She was continually surprised at how well her parents got along. They were total opposites yet they'd been married forty years and were still very much in love. She doubted she'd ever find a love as durable as theirs, one of the reasons she feigned lack of interest. As for the other reason, even her parents didn't know it. She'd never told them about the disastrous relationship she had while at college. She had come away from it more than a little the worse for wear. Having learned a bitter lesson, she'd convinced herself she would be happier on her own and had shied away from serious involvement. This approach had worked fine up to now.

The doorbell rang. Quinn turned to look as her mother emerged from the kitchen, taking off her apron and tossing it on the couch. She walked quickly through the living room to the front door.

"Hello, Louise, how are you tonight?"

Quinn could hear the deep, gravely voice greeting her mother, but whoever it was, was just out of sight around a corner. *Here comes trouble,* she groaned silently.

She thought she recognized the masculine voice though she couldn't quite place it. Her stomach did a little somersault. In spite of her determination to resist her mother's matchmaking, a small thrill of anticipation surged through her.

Then, as her mother and the stranger came into the living room, she caught sight of a familiar face. *Oh no, not him!* Her mother was smiling up at a tall, good-looking man. Taller than Quinn, taller even than her father from the look of him, he towered over her mother. It was that blasted neighbor, the miserable so-and-so who had insulted Horatio and threatened him with the shovel.

Quinn wanted to run and hide, but it was too late. In any case, a thirty-five-year-old woman who was thoroughly independent and ran her own business didn't run from trouble. It would be ridiculous to let him get to her, she thought. She'd find a way to survive the evening in spite of feeling sick at the thought of sitting down to a meal with that tyrant.

The man looked over and nodded at her father.

"Howard, how are you tonight? Recovered from our fishing trip yesterday?"

Quinn noticed the genuine warmth in his voice. Obviously he was fond of her father. His eyes, which had continued to scan the room, lit on her and stopped dead. Even at a distance they burned right through her, all friendliness gone. His face became closed and stern. She couldn't tell what he was thinking but it didn't look good. She met his gaze defiantly, giving back as good as she got. Her mother beamed at everyone, totally unaware of the sparks flying between Quinn and her neighbor.

"Harley, I want you to meet our daughter, Quinn. Quinn, this is Harley Donaldson, our new neighbor. He bought the Walters' house next door."

Quinn nodded politely. No point letting her mother know they'd already met, and not under the best of circumstances. Hopefully Mr. Donaldson wouldn't say anything to her folks about what had happened earlier. Quinn hated a scene, and her mother would be upset if she knew about the previous confrontation between Quinn and Harley.

"Mr. Donaldson." Quinn inclined her head slightly.

"Call me Harley." He held out his hand and, reluctantly, Quinn put out hers in response. As they touched, a jolt of electricity passed through their palms. Quinn recoiled. What was that all about?

When she had been out in the garden Quinn hadn't really noticed how handsome her parents' new neighbor was; she'd been too angry. Now, as she looked into his eyes, she felt a traitorous response to his magnetic good looks. He was very tall, close to six foot six, she guessed. His thick, black hair showed a touch of gray at the temples, giving him a distinguished look. His eyes were a deep, piercing blue. She recalled that when he'd glared at her in the garden his icy look had chilled her. He was tanned and fit and seemed uncomfortable in his formal clothing, as though he'd be more at home in jeans and a sweater like her. He was a monster but an extremely handsome one.

Drat, why did hormones always get in the way of common sense? Quinn thought ruefully. The way she felt usually spelled disaster where men were concerned.

She experimented with a tentative smile, which he appeared not to notice. He removed his hand, causing her to shiver slightly. His grip had been so warm and inviting; now she felt the chill of reality creeping in. There should be a law against any one man having that much animal magnetism, she groused to herself.

"Come on in, Harley. Sit down; make yourself at home." Her mother practically fawned over him.

Quinn was embarrassed by her mother's behavior. Unless he was a complete idiot, it wouldn't take Harley long to figure out what Marjorie was up to. He crossed the living room and sat down opposite Howard. The two men were soon engrossed in a conversation about fishing, ignoring Quinn as they discussed the merits of live bait over lures.

Her mother scurried off to the kitchen to check on dinner, calling to Quinn over her shoulder, "Pour a glass of water for Harley and your father, Quinn."

Quinn went over to the buffet and poured four glasses of water. She used the opportunity while Harley was deep in conversation with her father, to study him further.

He looked vaguely familiar. Quinn felt perhaps they'd met before, yet she was sure they couldn't have. His face wasn't easily forgettable. She had to admit, rather grudgingly, he was devastatingly good-looking. She was accustomed to towering over men but, even seated, his imposing presence dominated the room. He reminded her of one of the heroes of the romance novels she secretly liked to read: big and bold, a pirate perhaps. All he needed was a patch over one eye or a tattoo on his bicep. Perhaps he *had* a tattoo, Quinn speculated mischievously, thinking she'd love to find out. She stifled a giggle. Just then Harley happened to glance up and catch her staring. She blushed and turned away.

Quinn let her mother carry the conversational ball during dinner while she sat back and listened. Marjorie plied Harley with food, all the while prying expertly into his private life. He would soon discover, as Quinn had, that her mother's dinners came with a price tag attached.

Although Harley must have realized Marjorie's highly personal questions were not motivated merely by idle curiosity, he indulged her. Quinn noticed how kind he was to her parents.

Through her mother's probing, Quinn learned Harley had owned his own computer software company back East, selling out recently at a handsome profit, which had allowed him to retire in comfort. He said he was kept busy doing consulting and a little writing from home, but for the most part, his time was his own.

All through dinner and her mother's grilling, Harley never once looked in Quinn's direction, not even to see if she was listening. On the one hand, Quinn was annoyed he was ignoring her. On the other, she silently chided herself for not dressing up for dinner. Then, as soon as the thought of dressing to please any man crossed her mind, she became even more put out.

Why were men so shallow, worrying only about how women looked, anyway? She didn't care what he thought of her. Then why did she find it upsetting in the extreme to be ignored by a man to whom she had taken such an instant dislike? Was it because he was so eligible, yet so obviously uninterested and unapproachable?

Harley was attentive to her mother. He listened with interest to her father's stories and even laughed at his bad jokes, but he never directed any comments or questions Quinn's way. She wasn't used to anyone usurping her parents' attention, then adding insult to injury by acting as though she were invisible. Her parents were so charmed they hadn't even noticed.

All of a sudden it dawned on Quinn what he was up to. So this was how he was getting even with her for Horatio's little mishap. How petty! Quinn seethed. *She* had been willing to forgive and forget but obviously *he* held a grudge. The nerve!

Dinner lasted forever. Even the excellent food couldn't lift Quinn's spirits. By the end of the meal, she had decided emphatically that she wasn't the least bit interested in this Harley character.

But that face! It *did* look familiar. Where had she seen it before?

As Quinn sipped her coffee, she stifled a yawn. She

had put in a long day at the store before driving to Duncan. Harley glanced over and caught her with her mouth open. *Wouldn't you know it,* she thought. *He ignores me all evening and when he finally deigns to look my way, my face is as contorted as a Halloween mask.*

Harley gave her a wicked little smile and announced to her mother that he thought it was time for him to be going. Finishing his coffee and brandy, he got up and said his good-byes, shaking Quinn's hand solemnly once again.

When the door closed behind him, the room was strangely empty. Quinn poured herself and her father a final cup of coffee and slumped in the chair opposite him. She was too tired to drive home. She decided to stay overnight and return to Victoria in the morning.

With petulant energy, her mother was banging pots and pans in the kitchen. Giving her father a wry smile, Quinn pulled herself out of the chair and went into the kitchen to help with the dishes.

"Honestly, Quinn, you're your own worst enemy," her mother tackled her as soon as she walked into the kitchen.

"What do you mean?" Quinn asked, waiting for the inevitable criticism that would follow.

"Look at you! You completely ignored my request to change into something pretty. And you sat there all through dinner without saying a word. Couldn't you at least have tried to be polite and interested in the conversation? How are you ever going to find a man if you behave like that?" her mother scolded.

"Whatever gave you the idea I was looking for one, Mother? In case you hadn't noticed, I'm quite happy

on my own," Quinn bristled. "And if I *was* looking,
Mr. Donaldson would not be the kind of man I'd
choose." Quinn had to be careful. If she showed any
interest her mother would seize on it and redouble her
efforts. She would never hear the end of it. Besides,
Quinn wasn't really attracted to Harley. So he'd made
her blood heat up a little. After all, she *was* a normal,
healthy woman. But when she'd seen what kind of
man he was, she'd quickly brought her hormones under control, and now she wasn't the least bit interested.
Right! And the moon is made of green cheese, too!

"Harley's a wonderful man, and he's so good to
your father," her mother protested. "They go fishing
and golfing together, and he even invites Howard over
to play chess. He's obviously well-off financially and
he's very refined and sophisticated. He's just the sort
of man I hoped you'd meet someday. How could you
possibly dislike him?"

"He hates dogs!" Quinn announced, then threw
down the tea towel she'd been using, and stomped out
of the kitchen, much to her mother's surprise. Why
did being around her mother always make her regress
to behavior more suited to an adolescent than a suc-
cessful businesswoman?

Walking into the living room, Quinn noticed her
father slumped in his chair, newspaper falling from his
grasp. For a moment her heart stood still, then she
realized he was only sleeping. She tiptoed past and
made her way to the spare bedroom at the end of the
hallway. The room, which was Quinn's when she
stayed with her parents, was a perfect illustration of
the vast difference between her mother and herself.
Decorated in pastels of dusty rose, mauve, and moss

green, the room was fussy and feminine with lacy curtains and deep flounces on the bed skirt and pillows. Everything matched. How could the woman who had decorated this room have raised a daughter like her?

Feeling discouraged and out of sorts, Quinn undressed and crawled between the cool, scented sheets. In a little while, when she heard her parents' bedroom door close, she got up and sneaked back into the kitchen to get Horatio, coaxing him through the living room to her bedroom. Her own private act of rebellion. Horatio sniffed all around the room, eyeing her parents' closed door as if he knew there'd be trouble if Quinn's mother caught him. Then he settled down beside the bed, content to guard his mistress as usual. Quinn smiled to herself. Horatio loved her just the way she was: jeans, no makeup, and no patience for her mother's manipulations. As long as she had Horatio, she didn't need anyone else, especially not someone like Harley Donaldson.

Chapter Two

Quinn woke to the smell of coffee brewing and bacon frying. For a moment she wondered who'd broken into her apartment and was cooking breakfast. Then, as she opened her eyes and saw the lacy curtains of her parents' guestroom moving slightly in the breeze coming through the partially open window, she knew it was her father, not a thoughtful burglar, in the kitchen. She jumped up, took a quick shower, and threw on her clothes.

Horatio was nowhere to be seen. He'd probably wandered out to the kitchen when he heard her father. She stripped the bed and remade it with clean sheets, then made her way toward the coffee.

" 'Morning, Dad. Breakfast smells great!" She glanced around the kitchen. "Where's Horatio?"

"I let him outside; he won't go far."

"Oh no!" Quinn ran to the back door, opening it

and hollering, "Horatio, come here!" No sign of him! She quickly slipped on and tied her sneakers and went out to the backyard, checking around the side of the house to see if she could spot him. Not there! Had he gone next door to Harley's? She'd have to take the bull by the horns and go check. She hoped against hope that Horatio had had the good sense not to tangle with him again, but common sense had never been his strong suit. He was a lot like his mistress in that regard; he had a highly developed nose for trouble.

As she peeked through the hedge that separated the two properties, Quinn spotted Horatio making a bee-line for the deck at the back of Harley's house. The deck was low to the ground, and Horatio jumped up easily and loped to the sliding patio door, which was partially open. *Oh, Horatio, no!* Quinn's hand came involuntarily to her mouth, and she held her breath.

"Horatio, come here," she coaxed in a loud whisper, but Horatio, who had a bad habit of pretending he was deaf when he didn't want to obey, didn't even glance up as he moved purposefully toward the open door and disappeared inside.

People said Old English sheepdogs were untrainable, but Quinn knew this wasn't true. A stubborn breed with minds of their own, they gave the impression of being a little thickheaded. After living with Horatio, Quinn knew that sheepdogs weren't at all stupid. They *chose* not to obey. More like cats than dogs in this respect, they alone decided if they would listen to their owners' suggestions. This was one of the reasons Quinn loved them above all other breeds, though Horatio's independence had proven troublesome and inconvenient at times just like her own. And this was one of those times.

At this precise moment her only interest was in getting hold of him and returning to her parents' before any serious damage was done.

Quinn raced down the side of the house looking for a gap in the hedge to climb through into Harley's yard. Drat! She was losing precious time. She ran along the hedge to the front yard, then around the end and back down the other side. Horatio was nowhere to be seen; he must still have been inside the house.

She crept quietly across the yard and onto the deck. As she stepped on the cedar planking, it creaked ominously. Freezing in her tracks, she waited to see if Harley would come storming out. All was quiet. She continued moving slowly forward, tiptoeing to the open doors and peeking inside.

Horatio was in the kitchen. He had the good grace to look up guiltily as he heard his mistress approach. The tail end of a piece of meat was dangling from his mouth. A couple of snaps of his jaws and it disappeared. Whatever had been planned for it before this moment was of no consequence. It had just become Horatio's breakfast.

"Horatio," Quinn hissed, "what have you done?" She crept into the kitchen and grabbed his collar. An empty Styrofoam package labelled TOP SIRLOIN STEAK lay on the floor, wrapping intact except for a small hole through which Horatio had managed to liberate the steak before gobbling it up.

Quinn picked up the package. Darn! What in the world had possessed him to do such a thing? He was often mischievous but he had never stolen food before. Of all the times for him to become a sneak thief.

All of a sudden it dawned on Quinn that she'd forgotten to feed Horatio supper the night before. No wonder he'd sneaked over to Harley's kitchen and stolen the steak. She grinned sheepishly. Too late to worry about it now. She had to figure out how she was going to repair the damage. Run and hide? Go back to her parents' and pretend it never happened? No, her conscience would never let her do that. Perhaps she could drive to the supermarket and buy a replacement steak and sneak it into Harley's kitchen before he discovered his was missing. Yes, that's what she'd do. If she were quick, he'd be none the wiser.

With great haste, she wiped off the counter, cleaning up a few drops of blood which had fallen from the package to the floor. Leading Horatio to the door and out onto the deck, she congratulated herself on her escape while trying to think of an excuse for her parents as to why she needed to rush to the store before breakfast.

Just as Quinn was creeping to the edge of the deck, she heard a noise and turned to look. Who had wandered into the kitchen dangling an empty coffee cup from his left hand? None other than Harley. Dressed in jeans and a T-shirt and looking even more devastatingly handsome than the night before, he had obviously just emerged from the shower, as he had a towel draped around his neck and his hair was damp and curly. He had shaved, inadvertently leaving a tiny dab of shaving cream under his left ear, which endeared him to Quinn more than his seeming perfection of the previous evening. Somehow it made him seem more human. Quinn prayed he wouldn't notice Horatio and her. All she wanted was to get back into her parents' yard undetected.

She almost made a clean getaway. But Horatio, the traitor, didn't seem to realize *he* was the trespasser. He let out a series of loud barks as if to warn Harley he had walked into forbidden territory.

Quinn prayed that the deck would open up and swallow them both. She cringed with every bark, but forced herself to keep walking and pretending not to see Harley. One more step and she'd be off the deck and around the corner of the house, out of sight.

The suspense ended as Harley's deep voice growled at her.

"To what do I owe the honor of a visit so early in the morning?" he asked in a voice loaded with sarcasm.

She turned and looked at him, as guiltily as if it had been she who'd devoured his steak. "Good morning. I . . . uh . . ."

"What's that canine mop been up to now?" He sneered at Horatio.

"I'll thank you to not insult my dog." Quinn turned to confront Harley, trying desperately to forget that she should be apologizing instead of getting riled.

"Well, keep him out of my sight," Harley grumbled.

"I'm sorry. My father let him out of the house without thinking. I'll take him home right now," Quinn explained contritely.

The mention of Mr. O'Connell pacified Harley somewhat, and they both stood glaring at each other, saying nothing. Then all of a sudden Harley noticed the empty meat package in Quinn's hand.

"Where did that come from?" he asked, pointing to the Styrofoam tray. He turned and checked the counter where he'd left his steak to thaw, realized it was no longer there, and turned back to Quinn and Horatio, who was straining against his collar to free himself from her grip.

"Of all the . . ."

"Don't blame Horatio; it's completely my fault," Quinn said quickly. "I forgot to feed him last night. I guess he was hungry and smelled the meat. I was just going to go to the store and buy a replacement."

"That won't be necessary," Harley said, and Quinn thought she saw the beginnings of a smile flicker across his face, but it disappeared before she could be sure. A frown replaced whatever kindness had tried to surface.

"Just keep that poor excuse for a dog out of my yard. I don't ever want to see him again."

He turned and walked swiftly into the house, closing the door with a loud click. To add insult to injury, he drew the curtains, leaving Quinn staring at the house like a naughty child who'd just been caught throwing a rock through a neighbor's window.

She turned and walked quickly back to her parents', detouring long enough to lock Horatio in her car on the way.

"We'll have no more of your shenanigans, young man. You stay here and behave yourself till it's time to go home," she scolded him, trying to sound stern but all the while seeing the humor in the situation.

Her father was just finishing breakfast when she returned to the kitchen. He took a plate of pancakes out of the oven for her.

"Quinn, what's going on?" her mother called from the bedroom. "I thought I heard voices."

"I was talking to your neighbor, Mother."

Her mother completely missed the sarcasm in her voice.

"That's more like it. I knew you two would hit it off, if you gave him half a chance. He's an avid reader, just like you."

"We didn't talk about books." Quinn changed the subject quickly to avoid an inquisition. "I have to get back to Victoria right after breakfast. Are you going to come out, so I can say good-bye?"

Marjorie emerged from the bedroom dressed in a pretty green pantsuit with a flowered silk blouse, ready to face whatever the day would send her way. Quinn looked down at her faded jeans and shrugged, resigning herself to feeling like Cinderella, but with no handsome prince in sight. She polished off her breakfast and got up to kiss her mother.

"Your visits are always so short, Quinn," her mother complained good-naturedly. "Will we see you again next weekend?"

"I don't know, Mother. I'll call you." Not likely she'd dare come back for a while. She didn't want to risk another run-in between Horatio and Mr. Harley Donaldson.

Quinn hugged her father, told him not to overdo it, and beat a hasty retreat to the car, where Horatio greeted her lovingly, licking her ears as she buckled herself into the driver's seat. Sitting in the back seat just behind her, his big head almost touched the roof of the car.

"Lie down, Horatio, there's a good boy. You sure

got me in a heap of trouble, you devil. I hope you enjoyed that steak." Quinn chuckled at the memory of Horatio standing in Harley's kitchen with the steak dangling from his mouth. "You won't be needing any more meals today, you rascal." She ruffled his fur affectionately.

Horatio wagged what was left of his tail, which had been docked according to custom when he was only a few days old.

In England, where the sheepdog had been used for herding in days gone by, the tail of a dog was docked to show it was a working dog. That meant the owner didn't have to pay a tax on the animal. The custom had continued to the present, even though the vast majority of Old English sheepdogs, or bobtails as they were sometimes called, were bred for show or family pets. Recently Quinn had learned the custom had been outlawed in England, as it was deemed cruel. She wondered idly if the next generation of sheepdogs would sport long, shaggy tails. She tried to imagine Horatio with yet another appendage to get in the way, and laughed out loud.

Quinn quickly found the highway and headed back home to Victoria. Visiting her parents was at the very least exhausting and sometimes downright depressing. She came away feeling she'd let them down. She hoped they didn't find out what Horatio had done. Her father would get a chuckle out of the incident, adding it to his repertoire of stories, but her mother had such high hopes for a match between her new neighbor and Quinn that she would be terribly disappointed.

As she drove along, Quinn had a fleeting thought. Perhaps her parents were right. Maybe it was time for her to think about marriage. If she didn't marry soon, she might end up a lonely old woman. Perhaps she should take a look at that book, *The Spinster's Dilemma,* after all. Then she quickly came to her senses. *Quinn, give your head a shake. You've got the bookstore, lots of friends, and a busy life. And above all you've got Horatio. You'll be fine.*

Why then did she have a sad feeling creeping over her like a mist over water? Was it because of her father's comments about wanting grandchildren, or was it a result of her mother's attempts to pair her up with yet another eligible bachelor?

What a disaster dinner had been! Was it because she was unattractive that Harley had found it so easy to ignore her? Quinn bet she could get any man she wanted, even Harley Donaldson, if she put her mind to it.

If she got desperate, there was always good old Douglas, her high school friend, to fall back on. They had kept in touch over the years and, of late, had begun dating. The trouble was Douglas took the relationship much more seriously than Quinn. He wanted to marry her; he'd asked her dozens of times. But she didn't feel the least bit romantic toward him. Although he was a good friend, he didn't make her heart beat faster. When he kissed her, she found her thoughts wandering to the store's accounts or the book order she was expecting. If she had been going to fall in love with Douglas, she would have done it long ago.

Quinn had this crazy idea that if and when she *did* fall in love, it would be like being hit by a bolt of lightning. That was the way it happened in all the romance novels she'd ever read. Hero and heroine were swept away by love, coming together because they couldn't stay apart, not because they felt like comfortable old shoes together.

That was why she had always said no to Douglas when he popped the question. Perhaps she should reconsider. Maybe she could fall in love with him *after* they were married. Maybe what she was longing for didn't exist, except in romance novels. After playing around with the subject for several miles, Quinn reached a decision. No, she concluded firmly, Douglas wasn't the man for her. Better to stay single than marry an old shoe.

Quinn concentrated on her driving and was soon engulfed in the city, heading straight for James Bay, the pleasant old neighborhood where her apartment, in a renovated Victorian mansion, was located. She pulled into the driveway and let Horatio out of the back seat, locking the door behind him.

When she went inside the apartment, the blinking light on the answering machine caught her attention. She put Horatio out for a run then pushed the machine's button to listen to the messages.

"Quinn, Douglas here." While listening to the message, she took off her jacket and went into the kitchen to put a bowl of fresh water out for Horatio. No need to make him any supper after all the steak he'd eaten that morning.

"I have two tickets for the symphony at the Royal Theatre on Saturday night and thought you might like to go. How about dinner first? Give me a call."

The symphony sounded tempting. Before deciding whether to return Douglas's call, Quinn listened to the second message.

"Quinn, it's Mother. Harley called for you just after you left. When I told him you'd gone back to Victoria, he asked for your phone number. I gave him the number at the store. I hope you don't mind. And Quinn, try to be pleasant when he calls," her mother's voice pleaded. "Give him a chance."

Why did the message from Douglas leave her bored while the one from her mother made her heart race? This was ridiculous. There could be any number of reasons why Harley Donaldson had asked for her phone number. Perhaps he wanted to tell her how much it had cost to repair the damage Horatio had done the day before, or maybe he wanted to order a book. Why then was her hand trembling and her heart racing?

Quinn tried to talk herself out of the way she felt. *Don't be silly*, she argued. *Douglas may be boring, but at least he and Horatio like each other. Give him a chance. Don't even think about getting embroiled with Harley. Besides, he's not interested, remember?*

She quickly dialed Douglas's number. No answer. She left a message saying she'd love to go to the symphony and dinner sounded great too. She made up her mind to start taking him more seriously.

With that depressing thought uppermost in her mind, she gave the apartment a quick tidying up, then drove to the store to put together a book order. Afterward, feeling tired, she came back home and got ready for bed, setting her alarm for 7:00. Horatio was curled up on the mat beside the bed snoring lightly as she turned out the light.

Chapter Three

When the phone rang at the bookstore the next day, Quinn picked it up and answered without thinking. She had forgotten all about her mother's call.

"Words Unlimited," she said absentmindedly.

"Ms. O'Connell? This is Harley Donaldson. We met at your parents' on Saturday."

"Yes, I remember," she replied wryly. How could she forget? She hadn't been so embarrassed for a very long time, nor so disturbed by the mere presence of a man.

"What can I do for you, Mr. Donaldson?"

"You can start by calling me Harley," he said mildly.

"We went through this the other night, I seem to recall. I will, if you'll call me Quinn."

"I was wondering if you had the new mystery by

Peter Townsend in stock? Everyone seems to be sold out of it here in Duncan."

"As a matter of fact I do. Would you like me to send it to you? Perhaps you'd be willing to accept the book as payment for a certain piece of steak," she added mischievously.

"Actually I'll be in Victoria tomorrow. Perhaps I could drop by the store and pick it up? And I insist on paying for it. I told you not to worry about the steak."

"I'll put the book aside for you then. Do you know where the store is located?"

"Yes, I've been there a few times, even before I knew you were the owner," he said in a playful tone, "and I usually manage to find what I'm looking for, I might add."

"I'm happy to hear it." Why was he being so nice? Quinn was suspicious. "Is there anything else you need?" she asked briskly, wanting to get off the phone so she could collect her thoughts.

"Actually, there *is* something, but I'll save it until we see each other. I should be down in the early afternoon. Until then."

He hung up abruptly, leaving Quinn wondering what else he could possibly need from her. Another book? No, he would have mentioned it when he was ordering the Townsend book. He had been so dismissive and, at times, downright unpleasant when they'd met. She hoped it didn't have anything to do with Horatio's rather unruly behavior of the weekend. She made up her mind she wasn't going to take any flack from him. But she *would* tread lightly. She didn't want to upset her parents or cause unpleasantness between them and their new neighbor. He seemed to be good for her father. And her mother had such high hopes. Too bad she was going to be disappointed.

The day passed quickly, with an order of books delivered in the early afternoon and customers coming and going, keeping her busy until closing time.

The next day, Quinn dressed with extra care to go in to work. When she realized what she was doing, she feebly tried to explain to Horatio how it didn't hurt to wear a skirt and put on a little makeup once in a while, but he was unconvinced. He jumped up and licked her face, spoiling her carefully applied blush and putting her anxiety in perspective.

"You're absolutely right, old boy. 'Much ado about nothing,' as Shakespeare said."

Quinn felt nervous, but couldn't exactly say why. After all, she didn't even like Harley, did she? He *was* very handsome and well off and he *was* good to her father and he *did* make her heart beat faster, much faster than Douglas, but that didn't mean she liked him, did it?

As Quinn drove to the store, she had a crazy thought, so crazy she should have dismissed it immediately but she didn't. What if, she speculated, she decided to set her sights for Harley? What if she deliberately set out to attract his attention and interest? If she could get him interested in her, she could get her mother off her back, have a little fun, and pay him back for being so horrible to Horatio. She'd have her work cut out for her, though. He'd been downright rude when she chased Horatio out of his kitchen.

It would be a real challenge to topple Harley off his

high horse. But what a boost to her ego it would be, if she could get him to like her. Having to deal with her mother's constant efforts to find her a husband had played havoc with her self-esteem. She was feeling battered and bruised. This would give her a chance to get some of her own back, show Harley and her mother both a thing or two.

The only problem was that Quinn didn't know if she could pull off that kind of stunt, even on someone as miserable as Harley; he wasn't a bad person, just obnoxious and overbearing. Even *he* didn't deserve to be treated that badly. She made up her mind to see what he had on his mind. She promised herself if he was as unpleasant with her as he had been with Horatio, she just might set out to charm him, bring him to his knees, and then drop him like a hot potato. It would serve him right.

With that cheerful thought lingering in her mind, she perked up and spent a pleasant morning chatting to customers and tidying shelves. She set out a new book by her favorite author, Herbert Davis, writer of epic romances, on display. She had read all his other books and was looking forward to this latest one, which was supposed to be a real sizzler. She turned the book over and looked at the jacket. Now there was a handsome man! Pity the picture was such a poor one; it was blurred and hard to make out. The writer was sitting quite a distance from the camera in a garden. What had drawn him to Quinn's attention was the biggest, most beautiful sheepdog she'd ever seen sitting beside him. Most beautiful next to Horatio, that is.

She thought again of Harley. Too bad he didn't like dogs. If he did, she might have considered him as a serious candidate for her affections. But for Quinn, it was a case of "love me, love my dog." She could never seriously consider any man who didn't like animals and especially Horatio. She tucked a copy of the book under the counter to take home and read in bed that night. One of the perks of owning a bookstore was that she got to read all the latest books as they hit the market. This made up for some of the negatives: long hours, uncertain income, and hard, hard work. It was a small price to pay for being surrounded by books and being her own boss.

The bell over the door jingled and Quinn looked up from her reverie. A large figure stood in the doorway, blocking the sun and temporarily blinding her. She felt momentary panic until the stranger spoke and she recognized that familiar, deep drawl.

"Ms. O'Connell."

"Oh, it's you, Harley." *Be still my beating heart.* "I thought we agreed on first names."

"Quinn, *you* look very nice today," Harley commented.

"What do you mean by that?" Quinn asked defensively. Feeling silly that she had dressed up in anticipation of his visit, she wondered if he realized what she'd done. She didn't want him to think she'd cleaned up her act for him, even if it were true.

"Just what I said; you look nice. I meant it as a compliment." He advanced into the store.

A loud bark issued forth from the far corner.

"Horatio, it's okay, boy." Quinn turned apologetically to Harley. "Sorry, but he's very protective. And his memories of his previous meetings with you aren't exactly pleasant." She smiled, trying to provoke a laugh or at least a smile from her visitor.

"No?" Harley's eyebrows raised quizzically. "I would have thought his memory of our last meeting in particular would be very pleasant. He seemed to enjoy my steak enormously." Harley smiled ever so slightly.

"That's true, but, if it's any consolation, he suffered for it afterward. Beef doesn't agree with some sheepdogs and Horatio's one of them." Quinn turned to Horatio, who had risen and come to stand next to her. "Aren't you, Horatio?"

Horatio licked Quinn's hand, his stub of a tail trying its best to wag. Then he wandered over to Harley who abruptly turned away and began looking around the store. Quinn called Horatio back and told him to lie down, feeling hurt that Harley did not attempt to make friends with her best buddy.

"I have that book at the counter for you," she said abruptly. "Is there anything else I can get you?" She reached down and pulled out the first book her hand touched. "Here it is." She handed it to him without checking the cover.

"What's this, *The Happy Captive*? This isn't the book I ordered. I wanted Peter Townsend's new mystery. This is a romance." Harley spat out the last word as if he'd just discovered he'd bitten into a rotten apple.

Quinn blushed. "Oops, sorry. I gave you the wrong one. I'm holding that new Herbert Davis romance to take home."

"Don't tell me *you* read romances? You don't strike

me as the kind of woman who would enjoy hearts and flowers."

Quinn bristled at his condescending tone. "You have no idea what kind of woman I am. Furthermore, I don't know why you're belittling romance novels. Millions of women enjoy reading them. And Herbert Davis's books are some of the best on the market today. He's one of my favorite romance writers. At least *he* understands a woman's feelings, not like some men I could mention. Perhaps if men were a little more romantic in real life, women wouldn't have to look for romance in books. And besides, Mr. Davis likes sheepdogs. Not like you, Mr. Donaldson!"

Quinn's chest heaved and her eyes were fiery. She turned her back on Harley, found the Townsend book he had requested, and began to ring in the sale, leaving him standing with his mouth agape. She had been going to refuse payment for the book, but she was irked enough by his comments that there was no way she would make the gesture.

"My, aren't we touchy?" he said mildly. "I didn't mean to insult you and the millions of other women who read Herbert Davis. I was merely trying to say that I prefer a good mystery and would rather read the Townsend book." He handed the romance back to her, and she returned it to its place under the counter.

There was an awkward silence as Quinn considered what he had said.

"By way of apology, let me buy you dinner this evening. I know a nice little Greek restaurant not far from here. We could meet there after you close the store. I should be finished my errands by then."

"That's not necessary." Quinn's feelings were still

hurt. "Besides, I have to take Horatio home after work."

"I know it's not necessary, but I'd like to take you to dinner," he insisted. "There's something I want to discuss with you. It's too complicated to talk about here where we might be interrupted. We can meet a little later if you like, so you have time to take the dog home and freshen up. Not that you don't look perfectly presentable as you are," he added hurriedly, perhaps hoping to avoid another confrontation, "but I know how women like to fuss." He gave her a slightly superior smile that made her see red again.

"I hate fussing!" Quinn almost shouted, then realized she was being very rude over a trivial remark. She also remembered her as yet undeveloped plan to make Harley fall for her. She softened her approach just a little. "I guess I can meet you. Would six-thirty be all right? Which restaurant are you referring to? There are several Greek restaurants in the downtown area."

"Since you're planning to go home first, why don't I pick you up? That will save having to find parking for two vehicles."

"Okay," she agreed reluctantly. She gave him her address, and he paid for the book, saying he'd see her later. When the bell above the door signaled his departure, she collapsed into a nearby chair.

What an infuriating man! Even though she didn't want to like him, she felt immensely attracted to him on a physical level. How dare he say she wasn't the romantic type! He had no idea how she felt; they had only met a couple of times, and he couldn't possibly judge her character or her feelings by those meetings, which had been unusual, to say the least.

She made up her mind then and there to show him just how romantic she could be. She smiled wickedly. It might be kind of fun to see if *he* had any romance in his soul.

When the store closed that evening, Quinn raced home with Horatio, fed him his supper, and put him outside while she took a shower and dressed for her dinner date with Harley. She tried on three dresses before she settled on a rather plain but attractive kelly green dress with a flared skirt that showed off her long slim legs. The dress set off the rusty highlights in her hair. She slipped on a pair of shoes with two-inch heels. For once she didn't have to worry about towering over her date. Douglas was only an inch taller than she so she always wore flat shoes when they went out. The male ego was so fragile.

The doorbell rang just after 6:30. Quinn opened the door and was confronted by Harley holding a rose in his hand. He held it out to her, bowing slightly.

"Good evening, Quinn. I took your comments about romance to heart. This is my way of making amends for my tactless remarks. Will you forgive me?"

He smiled engagingly and it struck Quinn that this was the first time she'd noticed he had a dimple in his left cheek. It just wasn't fair for one man to be so good-looking!

"Thank you, Harley." She smiled in spite of herself. "Apology and rose accepted. Come on in and sit down while I find a vase. I'll be right with you." She led him into the living room, noticing a fluffy ball of dog hair in the corner and wishing she'd had a chance to tidy up the apartment before he arrived. Then, remembering how much she hated housework, she put the irksome thought out of her head. No way would she fuss around for him or any man. She went to the back door to call Horatio, who came bounding in, his face covered in dirt.

"What have you been up to?" she scolded. "You'll just have to stay like that until I come home. I don't have time to clean you up now. Go lie down on your mat," she said sternly, then relented, giving him a pat and a biscuit.

He ignored her admonition to stay on his mat and made a beeline for the living room. Before she had time to call him back she heard Harley swearing and saw Horatio come running back into the kitchen.

"Now what?" she called out to Harley, then as she went into the living room, she saw the reason for Harley's anger. He was brushing ineffectually at a big, black smudge on his tan slacks. Horatio.

"I'm sorry. Let me see if I can get that mark off for you." She grabbed a cloth from the kitchen and knelt down in front of Harley. The mark was just above the knee. She took hold of the material and rubbed hard, brushing against him in the process.

"I think *I'd* better do this," he said, looking down at her.

"Oh, you're so infuriating," Quinn snapped, standing up and tossing the cloth at him. "Here, clean it yourself."

Harley laughed at her discomfort and asked where the bathroom was. He came back into the living room in a moment. "There, I think I got it all. My pant leg is a little damp but it's warm out. It will dry quickly. Let's get out of here before that mutt of yours does any more damage."

"You seem to have a very negative effect on him. No one else has this problem. He's usually very obedient and well-behaved," Quinn said, her fingers crossed behind her back. That wasn't exactly the whole truth but darned if she'd let him insult Horatio without coming to his defense.

"If you hadn't told me, I would never have guessed. Never mind, let's not argue."

Quinn wondered what dinner would be like if they couldn't spend more than a few minutes in each other's company without fighting. She decided to make one final effort to be polite.

"Would you like to see the apartment before we go?"

"I made the reservation for seven, so we only have a few minutes. Sure, why not? Your taste is very different from your mother's."

Quinn felt her feathers ruffle yet again. Why was she always being compared to her mother? And why did she feel her mother bested her each time? She bit her tongue and said nothing. If she got into another argument with him before they even left the house, dinner was doomed to be a failure.

She led him through the house, pointing out the wainscoting in the dining room and hallway, the quaint bathroom with its pedestal sink and claw-foot tub, the ornate, vintage light fixtures.

"This is a beautiful old house, Quinn. I've always loved old homes. You've done wonders with it."

"Thank you, I love it too. An old house has so much character, don't you think?"

So they *could* be civil with each other, she thought. "Just let me get a wrap before we go." She grabbed a shawl from the bedroom and put it around her shoulders.

"All set?" he asked, eyeing her appreciatively.

Harley waited as she locked the front door and set the security system. They drove to the restaurant in his Mercedes. The top was down, and Quinn was reminded of parades she had seen as a child, with beauty queens riding in convertibles, waving to the crowds along the parade route. She sat a little straighter and was tempted to wave to some people who happened to look up as the Mercedes passed.

Harley drove alongside the harbor past the stately old Empress Hotel. A breeze coming from the water ruffled Quinn's hair and sent a shiver through her.

"Cold? There's a blanket on the backseat. Throw it over your lap," Harley said.

"No, I'm fine," she said, wrapping her shawl a little more tightly around her. "It can't be far. I know all the Greek restaurants in town and the best ones are only a few blocks from here."

Harley pulled up in front of the Apollo Restaurant and let her out to wait for him while he parked the car. How did he know this was her favorite spot? The restaurant was owned by a young family who'd taken it over a few years ago, about the time she'd bought Words Unlimited. Since the restaurant was close to the bookstore and served delicious, reasonably priced food, she was a regular customer. The staff knew her by name and often gave her a doggy bag for Horatio, with scraps of lamb or a bone for him to chew.

"Is this all right?" Harley asked as he walked up to where she stood waiting.

"More than all right. It's my favorite."

"So we *do* have something in common."

"I always have the hummus and pita, then a Greek salad and a side order of calamari. What about you?" Quinn asked.

"For me, it's the hummus, followed by the roast lamb."

"Oh, that's okay then. I was worried we'd be ordering the same dishes," Quinn teased. "I always get after Mother and Dad for doing that. Dad says it's because they've lived together so long."

"I agree with your dad. My parents do it too," Harley replied.

Theo, the owner, seated them in a dimly lit corner of the restaurant and struck a match, holding it to the candle on their table. He brought a pitcher of iced tea without being asked, pouring two glasses. He winked at Quinn and gave her the thumbs-up signal behind Harley's back, making her smile.

Theo didn't approve of Douglas. He'd told her time and time again, "The man has no romance in his soul. He should be able to make your heart sing, and if he doesn't, he's not for you." If he thought Douglas wasn't romantic, what would he think of Harley, who was so disdainful of romance novels and the women who read them?

"To us." Harley raised his glass and held it out to clink against Quinn's.

"Don't you think that's a little premature? We've just met. We barely know each other," Quinn protested, unwilling to touch her glass to his and complete the toast.

"Actually, I feel as if I know you quite well. Your parents talk about you all the time. They're very proud of you."

Quinn looked up from her drink in surprise. What had her parents been saying to Harley? She hadn't realized they were so proud of her. She was so certain she had failed to meet their expectations. Once again her face reddened. It was starting to become a habit around this man.

"Well, I don't know anything about you," she said to cover her confusion. "I didn't even know you existed until last Saturday," she protested.

"I beg to differ," Harley said smoothly. "After your mother's inquisition at the dinner table Saturday night, you should be able to write a pretty accurate biography of me without much trouble." He chuckled and sat back, waiting to see how Quinn would react.

She started to feel embarrassed and defensive, then the humor of the situation struck her, and she laughed instead.

"What's so funny?" Harley studied Quinn's smiling face.

"My mother—she never gives up. She's always trying to match me with eligible bachelors: her friends' sons, the local doctor, her accountant. Don't flatter yourself. You're just the latest in a long list of contenders, and I'm sure you won't be the last," Quinn asserted, attempting to knock Harley down a peg or two.

Harley muttered something under his breath. It sounded like, "don't be so sure," but Quinn couldn't be certain. She must have misunderstood.

"I wasn't going to bring this up until a little later, after I had plied you with food, but I have a proposition for you. Since you've introduced the subject, I may as well ask you now."

She frowned at him. What kind of woman did he think she was?

"It's nothing like that," he said quickly. "Your reputation is safe with me. It's about your mother and my mother and what we can do to get them both off our backs."

"What do you mean?" What was he hinting at? She studied his face, but could find no clue as to what he meant.

"I'd be willing to bet you don't find it pleasant having your mother drag every Tom, Dick, and Harry home for dinner, trying to marry you off. Believe it or not, I have the same problem. My mother and sisters are forever prying into my love life, wanting to know when and whom I am going to marry. I'm getting a little tired of fighting off desperate women who are afraid of being left alone or worried their biological clocks will run down before they find a man to father their children. I'm tired of having to explain I'm perfectly happy the way I am." Harley sat back in his chair and took a sip of his wine.

"My sentiments exactly! But what do you propose to do about it?" What was he getting at?

"I suggest we tell our mothers we're dating each other—become a couple in the eyes of the world. This will satisfy both families and leave us free to enjoy our single lives. What do you say?"

Quinn was stunned. For a brief moment, when Harley had invited her for dinner, she had thought he was interested in her. She hadn't suspected he wanted to use her as camouflage. He had no feelings toward her other than wanting to use her to keep his family from harassing him about marriage.

Then she thought about what she had been planning to do and realized it wasn't much different. It would serve him right if she accepted his offer. She raised her glass to her lips and looked around the restaurant, determined not to let him see her hurt feelings.

"I'll have to think about it," she said coolly. "I can tell you one thing. The whole thing would have to be very convincing or my mother would sniff out the plot like a bloodhound. I don't know if it's such a good idea." She frowned.

"Where's your spirit of adventure? I'll bet situations like this have appeared in some of those romance novels you're so fond of. Don't they always end happily ever after? What harm can there be in this?" he insisted.

"You're right. I have read of similar arrangements. Usually one or the other of the couple ends up falling in love and being heartbroken until the hoax is discovered. Then they fall in love in earnest. It doesn't sound at all like our situation."

"No, we won't have to worry about falling in love," he agreed. "You're not the least bit attracted to me and I'm not attracted to you. I think you're very nice," he added hurriedly, "but you're not my type."

Quinn's eyes flashed. She wasn't about to admit she

found him attractive, especially after he'd just said he
didn't find her appealing. But she wondered who *was*
his type anyway? She made up her mind. It was as if
he had thrown down the gauntlet. She had never refused a dare before, and she wouldn't refuse his challenge now. If he could handle it, so could she. She
wouldn't be the one to end up with a broken heart.

"Okay, I'll do it," she decided quickly, hoping the
spark of interest in her eyes was disguised by the flickering candlelight. "But on one condition. If either of
us decides it isn't working out as we thought, we'll
call the whole thing off. And we mustn't hurt our families. After all, we don't want to upset them, just trick
them into leaving us alone."

She hadn't realized how tense he'd been. But as she
outlined her condition, he relaxed visibly, saying
quickly, "Agreed. I like your parents very much and I
wouldn't want to hurt them." He paused for a minute,
and she wondered what was coming next. "Now that
that's settled, what about other men and women?"

"What do you mean?" Quinn regarded him with a
puzzled look, placing her wineglass on the white linen
tablecloth with more care than was warranted. She
looked up quickly, hoping to catch him off guard and
read his emotions, but no such luck. He was studying
her intently, his composure masking his feelings.

"To make this charade look real, I don't think either
of us should go out with other men or women. Is this
a problem for you?" he asked casually.

"I have a dinner engagement on Saturday, but after
that it should be fine. They're not exactly breaking
down my door." She laughed, relieved. She was glad
his response was so straightforward.

"I didn't know there was a man in your life." Harley frowned. "Your parents never mentioned him."

"Douglas is just a friend. What about you?" she questioned.

"There was someone, but I've been looking for a reason to break it off. She's starting to get much too serious. This will give me the excuse I need. We'll start Saturday, then." He sat back, seemingly satisfied by their agreement.

"Not so fast, mister. Now that we've got that out of the way, there's one more thing we have to discuss."

Now it was Harley's turn to look puzzled and just a little apprehensive.

"What about Horatio?" Quinn demanded, pleased to have caught him off guard.

"What about that canine disaster?" he asked, still puzzled.

"There you go again. That's exactly the problem. My parents will know right away there's something fishy if you continue to make remarks like that. They know I could never be serious about anyone who doesn't like Horatio," she insisted.

"Well . . ." He paused and studied her to see if she was serious. "I'll try, but I can't promise he and I are going to become the best of friends. I'm not crazy about sheepdogs. They're so big and hairy," he added, feebly casting about for an explanation to justify his dislike. "I prefer a short-haired breed like the boxer or lab. But I'll try." He paused, then added, "I promise," as if she might not believe him.

"Okay, that's settled, then." Quinn decided to accept his word and hold him to it.

"To us," Harley repeated the toast he'd made at the beginning of the evening, and this time Quinn raised her glass and clinked it against his. She spotted Theo smiling over at them and her heart sank.

Chapter Four

When Quinn woke up the next morning she lay in bed for a few moments mulling over events of the previous night. She had wondered if she'd feel differently, knowing that soon everyone would think she and Harley were an item. After taking time to reflect, she decided she didn't. Nothing had changed and nothing would until after her weekend date with Douglas.

She wasn't looking forward to it. She'd have to tell him she wasn't going to see him anymore, that she'd met someone else. In a way, this was a good thing. He'd hung around all these years, hoping her feelings would change. She had never had the courage to tell him once and for all that there was no hope for their relationship. Now he would know it was over and he should find another woman to shower with affection. He would make some woman very happy; it just couldn't be her.

Her dinner with Harley had been surprisingly pleasant after they'd got the discussion of their courtship
out of the way. He was an entertaining companion,
regaling her with stories of his life in Toronto, before
he'd sold his business and moved out West. They had
lingered over dinner, ordering coffee and talking non-
stop until Theo had coughed politely and they'd finally
noticed that the restaurant's other patrons had long
since departed and the staff was waiting to close up.
Harley had paid the bill, leaving a substantial tip by
way of apology, and they'd returned to the Mercedes.
He'd put the top up as the evening had cooled and the
breeze off the ocean was brisk and he had driven
Quinn home. As she'd sunk comfortably into the
leather seat next to him, Quinn had thought about their
bargain, and wondered if she would be able to keep
her end of it. She found Harley disturbingly attractive.
Once they'd got past the unpleasantness of their dis-
putes over Horatio, he'd been charming and attentive.
Only time would tell whether she would be able to
keep their arrangement strictly business.

Harley didn't seem to be worried about maintaining
the relationship as it was. When they had arrived at
her apartment, she'd asked him if he wanted to come
in for coffee but he'd declined, saying he had a long
drive ahead of him. He'd walked her to her door,
shaken her hand as though she were a business acquaintance, and left immediately.

She felt a little disappointed. She decided it was
nothing some good, hard work couldn't cure. She
sprang out of bed and headed for the shower.

*   *   *

The day was bright and warm, with a cloudless, azure sky. The weather, although always a little unpredictable in Victoria, looked as though it would be perfect for the long weekend coming up in a few days. Locals said if you didn't like the weather, wait a few minutes and it would change. Too bad about her arrangement for dinner and the symphony with Douglas on Saturday. It would have been a perfect weekend for the season's first camping trip with Horatio.

Quinn ate breakfast, then fed Horatio and washed up the dishes before going to the store. It was going to be a busy day. Dani, Quinn's employee and friend, was back from a few days holiday, but had asked for the afternoon off to attend her nephew's graduation ceremony, and Quinn had agreed.

Dani, a single parent, had worked for Quinn since soon after she bought the store. She was energetic and hardworking and most important, always good-natured, even with the most difficult of customers. They had become close friends. In fact, Dani was the best friend Quinn had ever had. She was totally accepting of all her little quirks and foibles, of which there were many, and she was fun to be with.

Quinn wondered how Dani would take the news of her arrangement with Harley. There was no question of not telling her, even though Quinn and Harley had agreed to keep it secret. Dani would realize right away there was something going on. Though she had been telling Quinn for years to let Douglas go and move on, she would be suspicious that it had happened and that Quinn had become involved with someone else.

Dani would definitely not approve of their bargain.

She wanted Quinn to fall in love, not get involved in a silly pact where she only pretended to care.

Dani believed in love. In spite of difficulties in her first marriage, she had not become hard and cynical. She still believed there was a Mr. Right out there for each of them.

When Quinn thought about the unhappy relationship she'd had during her college days and compared it with what Dani had been through, she wondered what made two people react so differently to similar situations. Dani had bounced back believing that she would one day meet the man of her dreams, whereas Quinn had become cautious and cynical, unwilling to take a chance.

To be sure, Dani's optimism had suffered occasional setbacks, but recently she'd met a man who was, in Quinn's estimation, boring but dependable, and she'd fallen madly in love. Dani just laughed at Quinn when she said he wasn't very exciting and said she wasn't looking for excitement; she'd had enough to last her a lifetime. No, Dani would definitely not approve of Quinn's business arrangement with Harley.

When Quinn arrived at the store, Dani was already hard at work. That was another thing Quinn loved about Dani: she always got to work early and made the coffee. As she opened the door, she was greeted with the fragrance of the strong, dark brew Dani preferred and Quinn had grown accustomed to.

"Good morning, boss. How are you this bright spring morning?" Dani chirped.

"Enough already, you know I'm not at my best this early in the morning. Horatio, come on, come inside."

Horatio had discovered an intriguing scent and was sniffing around the curb in front of the store.

"Let's go," Quinn said impatiently. He finally looked up and followed her into the store, going straight to his mat in the corner.

"You seem even sleepier than usual this morning, Quinn. Didn't you have a good night?"

"I was out late last night, and no, I didn't sleep all that well."

"Was it Douglas again? Honestly, Quinn, when are you going to put that man out of his misery?"

"I wasn't out with Douglas last night, and to answer your second question, I plan to do just that Saturday night. We're going out for dinner and to the symphony. I'm planning to take your advice and tell him I can't see him anymore."

Dani smiled, showing the dimples in her round cheeks. "Well, it's about time! What finally prompted you to make the big move? It wasn't my advice, or you would have done it years ago. What's up?"

That was Quinn's ready-made cue to tell Dani about Harley, but for some reason she couldn't bring herself to confess just yet. In the harsh light of day, the whole situation seemed ridiculous. Besides, she wanted to keep the illusion alive a while longer, to pretend that Harley was a serious suitor. It would be downright embarrassing to admit that the only man she could attract was one who wanted to use her to trick his family into thinking he'd met someone special, so they would stop harassing him about marriage. She couldn't face Dani's outrage this early in the morning. No, she would wait a while, perhaps until she had an opportunity to introduce Dani to Harley before she told her the truth. After Dani had a look at him, she'd be more sympathetic.

"I decided you were right all along, though it pains me to admit it." Quinn smiled.

"Whatever the reason, I'm glad you've come to your senses. But why wait until Saturday? Here he comes now." She pointed out the window where Quinn spotted Douglas approaching. He was an optometrist, his office located just down the street from the bookstore. His habit was to drop by for coffee in the morning before his first appointment.

"Dani, don't you dare say a word," Quinn threatened. "I have to do this my way. I want to break the news gently, without hurting his feelings. Promise me you'll keep that big mouth of yours shut tight."

"What a party pooper! Okay, I'll shut up, but come Saturday, if you chicken out, I'll tell him myself." She turned toward the door as the bell rang. "Good morning, Sir Doug, and how are you this wonderful morning?"

"Good morning, Dani." Douglas could never quite comprehend when Dani was joking and when she was serious. He regarded her for a moment before smiling. The man had no sense of humor, one of the reasons Quinn couldn't consider him a serious suitor.

"Hi, Douglas, coffee's ready." Quinn poured a cup for herself and held up the pot, gesturing toward him.

"Not this morning, Quinn." He shook his head. "I have an early appointment. I just came by to see if you were busy later. I need to discuss something with you." He looked uneasy, not quite meeting her gaze.

"I can't meet you today. Dani's abandoning me this afternoon in favor of a dusty gymnasium and hundreds of young people in caps and gowns. Can't it wait until Saturday? We'll have time to talk over dinner."

"That's just it. I can't make it Saturday and I must talk to you as soon as possible. How about tonight, after supper? What I have to say can't wait."

"If it's that important, I'll make a point of staying home. I had planned to take Horatio for a walk around Elk Lake, but I can put it off for one more evening." Horatio lifted his head, then put it down again and closed his eyes. Quinn hoped he wasn't sick; he had seemed tired and listless since the weekend.

"I'll see you about seven then," Douglas said as he turned and walked away, not even glancing back.

"Hmm, that was strange. What does Sir Douglas want now? Is he getting ready to propose again? How many times will that make?" Dani joked.

"Don't make fun of him, Dani. You know he's a nice guy. I wonder what's up? He was acting strangely. Did you notice how he didn't look me in the eye? Or was I imagining things?"

"No, you weren't; I noticed it too. He definitely has something on his mind. But if not matrimony, what? Oh, I know; maybe he wants to borrow some money," she joked. Douglas's frugality was a standing joke between them. He hated to part with a penny and was scrupulous about calculating his share of the bill whenever he and Quinn went out.

"Somehow I don't think this is about money," Quinn mused.

Quinn's curiosity was piqued, but there was nothing to do but wait until that evening to find out what was bothering him. She busied herself around the store, which, after Dani left to attend the graduation, was steady with customers.

She thought about what Dani had said about Douglas and money. If anyone should be borrowing money, it was she, not he. Although the store was busy, she had noticed her sales dropping off for the past several months, ever since The Warehouse, a huge discount bookstore, had come to town. There were many small stores like hers in Victoria, and each had its own specialty and clientele. Until recently, they had naturally divided the available customers among themselves, all making a decent living. But since the arrival of The Warehouse, all the smaller stores were noticing a drop in sales, and Quinn's was no exception. She hadn't said anything to Dani, but if the trend continued, she would have to cut her hours, which she was loath to do. Dani had been a loyal employee, and she needed the money. This had been on Quinn's mind for some time and although she had been searching for another solution, so far, she hadn't found one.

She put her problems out of her mind as she served her last customer, closed up, and prepared to go home. She had to get supper and prepare for Douglas's visit.

The alarm on her wristwatch beeped seven times as the doorbell rang. Quinn smiled. Douglas was nothing if not punctual. He was almost too dependable and predictable, but she would miss him. She wondered if it would be possible for them to remain friends after tonight. For she had decided that after he told her whatever was troubling him, she would tell him she couldn't go out with him anymore. There was no point in waiting. She took a deep breath and opened the door.

"Hi, Douglas, how are you?" Quinn studied his face, then added, "You look a little glum." He had a decidedly unhappy expression. Why was it that this man who'd been so steadfast over the years wasn't able to make her heart beat faster? If she had married him, she would never have to worry about where he was or what he was doing. Good old Douglas, she would miss him.

"Quinn, let's sit down. We need to talk. This can't wait any longer." He frowned as he headed for the living room, plunking himself down on the sofa.

"You're beginning to scare me, Douglas, what's the matter? You're not sick, are you?" She sat down next to him.

He fidgeted with the button on his shirt, avoiding her gaze. "Quinn, there's no easy way to say this. I've met someone else. I won't be able to go out with you anymore." He paused as if to gather courage, then continued. "You and I have been seeing each other for a long time. I had hoped you would agree to marry me one day. I've been patient, hoping you'd realize we could be good for each other. But it hasn't happened, and I can't wait any longer."

Quinn felt as though Douglas had struck her. This was almost exactly what she had been planning to say to him. She couldn't believe Douglas was dumping *her*. She was the one who was supposed to be doing the dumping.

A feeling of panic came over Quinn, and she suddenly felt completely alone. Even Douglas, the one man she'd always felt she could fall back on, no longer wanted her. She took a few deep breaths to calm herself, then turned back to him. He was still talking and she'd lost the thread of the conversation. She picked it up as she heard him say,

". . . so you see, Quinn, it's time we both moved on. You remember I hired a new receptionist a couple of months ago? Trish and I have become quite close. The qualities in me that bore you—no, don't deny it, Quinn, you know it's true—Trish finds them desirable." He smiled an embarrassed little smile. "She's been bringing up her son on her own and is looking forward to having someone around to help. Quinn, are you listening?"

"What? Oh yes, Douglas, that's very nice," Quinn said halfheartedly. "I'm sure you'll both be very happy." She stood up hoping this would serve as a signal for him to leave. "Shouldn't you be getting back to Trish? I'm very happy for you, Douglas, honestly, just a little surprised, that's all." She tried to smile a bright cheerful smile, failing miserably.

"Well, if you're sure you're okay, I'd better get going. I hope we can remain friends." He gave her a hug, which in a way was good because it reminded her why this was happening. She felt confined by his arms and instead of prolonging the contact, wanted to push him away.

Quinn was numb as she hustled Douglas out the door. Even though he'd saved her the trouble of having to break off their relationship, she felt abandoned. A tear made its way from the corner of her eye down her face to her mouth and she licked it away. She'd lost a good friend. She and Douglas had been hanging around together for years and now, all of a sudden, he'd cut her adrift.

She pulled herself together as she remembered that what he'd said to her was exactly the same speech she'd been planning to give him. It only felt bad because Douglas, not she, had made the first move. She went to the telephone to call Dani. She'd promised her a full report. *Boy, will she ever get a good laugh at my expense,* Quinn thought.

Dani was too kind to laugh, though she was quick to point out that things couldn't have gone better, and after she explained several times why this was so, Quinn had to agree. When she hung up she felt better, as she always did after baring her soul to Dani.

Just as Quinn replaced the receiver, the phone rang. Glancing at her watch, she realized it was only 9:00, she had thought it much later. She picked up the receiver.

"Hello?"

"Hello Quinn?"

Her heart skipped a beat as she recognized the voice at the other end of the line.

"Quinn, is that you?"

"Yes. Hello, Harley."

"You sound upset; is everything all right?"

"Everything's fine. I'm just tired. What about you? Did you have a good trip home last night?"

"Yes, it was a beautiful night. I would have enjoyed it more if you'd been there with me, though."

Her heart did a somersault, but then she remembered he was just practicing for the time when he would pretend to be in love with her for the benefit of their families.

"Oh, I don't think that would have worked; I don't go anywhere without Horatio and somehow I just can't see you wanting him in your Mercedes," she replied testily.

"I'm not as much of an ogre as you think," he said, then changed the subject. "I just called to see if you've changed your mind about our agreement?"

"Don't worry, I have no intention of changing my mind. You'll be the one to cry uncle."

"What do you mean?"

"Never mind, it's not important." She felt dispirited and not in the mood for jokes.

"I was wondering if you were planning to visit your parents this weekend? Oh, darn, I just remembered your dinner date on Saturday."

"The date's been cancelled," Quinn said quickly. No need to tell Harley she'd been dumped. "Why do you ask?"

"Well, I was thinking it would be a good time for you to tell your parents about us."

"There isn't much to tell yet. I guess I could say you came to Victoria and took me out for dinner." Quinn wasn't anxious to tell her mother she was seeing Harley, as she knew what a fuss she would make.

"That's a good start. You could also tell them you find me handsome and exciting and are looking forward to getting to know me better." He chuckled wickedly.

"I don't want to lie outright!" Quinn laughed in spite of herself. "Just joking!"

"Are you ready to meet my family? My mother and sisters are coming over from Vancouver for the long weekend, and I thought I'd put on a barbecue and invite your parents. It would be the perfect opportunity for you to meet my family, and for them to meet you. What do you say?"

"There's no point in delaying the inevitable. I was thinking about coming up anyway, now that I don't need to be in town. I guess I can make it," she said grudgingly.

"Such enthusiasm!" Harley laughed at Quinn's reluctance. "Quinn, we can have fun with this. Let's just pretend that we really want to spend time together, and we'll enjoy our little game. I'll expect you around eight on Saturday night, and don't worry about dressing up. We'll be outside on the patio."

"Okay, good-bye." She hung up the phone and for the first time had misgivings about the practicality of their arrangement. He had caught her at a vulnerable time, and now, with Douglas gone, her situation had worsened, if anything. She wished she could talk to Dani, but couldn't bring herself to admit how big a fool she'd was, not even to her.

Chapter Five

"What are your plans for the weekend, Quinn?" Dani asked casually over morning coffee the next day.

Quinn hesitated. She had been planning to slip away after work on Saturday without telling Dani anything, but she really felt the need to talk. Depression had descended over her as she thought about her bargain with Harley. She made up her mind.

"I'm going to Duncan to visit Mother and Dad. And while I'm there, I'll be attending a barbecue at the next-door neighbor's."

"That sounds really exciting, Quinn," Dani said sarcastically. "Aren't the neighbors over eighty? It's time you found a new love interest and quit hanging around with your parents and their geriatric neighbors."

"The Walters have moved. The new neighbor is a very good-looking man, mid-forties, well off financially. He's got all the right qualifications. You'd approve."

"That's more like it!" Dani perked up. "Tell me all about him."

"I met him last weekend when I went to my parents' for dinner. He's my mother's latest attempt at finding me an eligible bachelor."

"Sounds like your mother finally found a live one," Dani joked. "Why so glum? I should have thought you'd be pleased."

"Oh, Dani," Quinn wailed, "I've really got myself into a mess. He tookme out to dinner the night before last and I kind of made this silly agreement with him. He wants us to pretend we're interested in each other to get our families to quit pestering us about marriage. The trouble is I find him very attractive, while he seems to just want to use me to trick his family," she said dejectedly.

"That's wonderful! I've been waiting for two years for the great and mighty Quinn to admit she might have real feelings. So, break the agreement and go after him in earnest," Dani said blithely, ignoring the gloomy expression on Quinn's face. "What's holding you back?"

"I can't break the agreement," Quinn explained in an exasperated tone. "Besides, he's not the least bit interested in me. And, to top it off, he doesn't like Horatio," Quinn added.

"Quinn O'Connell, give your head a shake," Dani scolded. "The man wouldn't have made this bargain with you unless he found you attractive. Would *you* want to be stuck in an arrangement like that with

Douglas or someone you didn't feel drawn to? No! He's using this as a way of getting you to go out with him." Dani sat back, looking as pleased as Punch at her conclusion.

"I don't think so, Dani," Quinn said slowly. "When we met last weekend, he ignored me completely. And you're forgetting something—he's not a dog lover. He's got it in for Horatio."

"Look, before I met Horatio, I wasn't a dog lover either. He kind of grows on you. I'm sure when this guy has a chance to get to know him he'll love him just like I do now. Horatio's such a sweetie and he's so well behaved."

Quinn laughed in spite of herself. "You know what he did last weekend?" She recounted what had happened when Horatio had met Harley, and how Horatio had stolen Harley's supper right out of his kitchen.

"So they got off to a bad start." Dani dismissed the information with a wave of her hand. She leaned toward Quinn and said earnestly, "Don't worry. If you like the guy, go after him. Everything else will fall into place. Now, when are you going to see him again?"

"Saturday at the barbecue. He wants me to meet his mother and sisters," Quinn admitted.

"That's a good sign," Dani said gleefully. "Now, we have lots of work to do before then. You've neglected yourself and your wardrobe terribly." Dani shook her finger at Quinn. "We have to find you something stunning to wear."

"Do we have to go shopping?" Quinn complained. "You know how I hate it." She glanced down at her faded jeans and T-shirt and realized that Dani was right. She really did need to pay some attention to her nonexistent wardrobe.

"Yes we do, and you're going to get your hair trimmed too. And look at those nails." Dani grimaced as she pointed at Quinn's hands. "When you see Harley Donaldson again, he won't recognize you. You'll sweep him off his feet."

"Not much chance of that. The man doesn't have a romantic bone in his body. But he's so handsome, who cares?" Quinn added, her good humor restored. It was impossible to be depressed around Dani. Both women burst out laughing, and Quinn vowed to let Dani help her. If she was going to bring Harley to his knees, she needed all the help she could get.

The rest of the week was a mad round of shopping for the two women. Dani took Quinn to her favorite hair stylist and gave him orders not to let Quinn out of the chair until she was transformed. She had a trim and soft perm, so that her short hair fell in waves around her face, softening her look. Then she suffered a manicure, a pedicure, and even a facial. By the end of the week, she felt thoroughly pampered and was even beginning to enjoy herself.

Quinn wondered if Harley would notice the change. She was nervous about meeting his family and wished she could come up with an excuse why she couldn't go to Duncan on Saturday. But there could be no backing down. Her mother had already called, thrilled that the three of them had been invited to Harley's to meet his family. Harley had told her he and Quinn had been out for dinner, and tried to pump Quinn for details but all Quinn would say was that it had been very pleasant and that he was quite nice. No way she could let her mother in on the truth. She would tell her parents that she and Harley were dating but she didn't want her mother to discover her true feelings. No one but Dani must know how she felt. Especially not Harley. He had to be convinced she was merely living up to their bargain. She would die if he knew she was attracted to him. She even thought she recognized the disagreeable symptoms of love overtaking her.

After Quinn closed the store on Saturday, she went home to pick up her overnight case, which was packed with all her new outfits. She would wait until arriving in Duncan to change into the flowing silk pantsuit Dani had insisted she buy to wear to the barbecue. It was cinnamon-colored with an abstract pattern in browns and beiges. The colors brought out the highlights in Quinn's hair. Even the nail polish she was wearing blended with the outfit. She had never before been so color-coordinated. It was downright scary!

As she drove to Duncan, Quinn became more and more agitated. What if Harley didn't like the new her? And what about his family—would they like her? She groaned out loud, causing Horatio to sit up and perk his ears. She never should have gotten herself into this phony relationship. It was too late to do anything about it tonight. But after the weekend, perhaps she would tell him she'd had second thoughts and wanted out of the agreement. After all, that was part of their bargain too. If one or the other of them decided it wasn't working, they could call it off.

She pulled into her parents' driveway. They had left the light on above the back door, but the house was dark. They must have already gone next door to the barbecue. Lights emanated from Harley's backyard and Quinn could hear the sound of music and voices. It seemed the party was in full swing. She let Horatio out of the car, grabbed her bag, and walked quickly to the house. She let herself in with her key.

"Horatio, you stay in the kitchen. I'm going to take a shower and get dressed and then I'll be back to make you some supper before I go to the barbecue."

Horatio looked up at Quinn reproachfully as if to say, "last time we were here you forgot to feed me." Then he lay down in the corner with his head on his front paws and closed his eyes. All she could see of his face was his shiny black nose.

She took her bag into the spare room and laid out her new clothes on the bed. She glanced at herself in the mirror. *Not bad,* she thought. Though she was tall and slim, Quinn had a good figure. Her skin was smooth and tanned.

Though she couldn't stand the idea of exercise for its own sake and never worked out, her work was quite physical, so she was in good shape.

It was hard to get time outdoors, being so busy in the store during the day. Nevertheless she glowed with good health.

She hopped into the shower and quickly lathered herself all over taking care not to wet her hair. She was still learning how to get it to fall nicely into place and didn't want to have to fuss with it when she was already late. She finished off the shower with a dose of cold water, then jumped out and rubbed herself all over, bringing a healthy pink tinge to her skin. She dressed quickly and then examined herself once again. She'd do. She ran a brush through her hair, sprayed some scent on her wrists, and went back through the living room to the kitchen.

"Horatio, you stay here. I'll be back soon." She quickly filled a bowl with water for him and put some dog food into a second bowl. "There, that should keep you busy while I'm gone." She bent down to give him a last pat and he looked at her mournfully. "No, you can't come with me." He stood waiting beside the door, as if he hadn't heard.

"I have to go now, Horatio. Be good."

She opened the door, and before she could slip out and close it behind her, Horatio made a break for freedom, disappearing around the side of the house and heading straight for Harley's.

"Horatio, come back!" Quinn called frantically after him. Darn! Why did he have to act up tonight? What was it about Harley's place that kept drawing him there? Then she realized even she could smell the steaks cooking on the barbecue. Horatio was no dummy. He knew where to find good eats. Why be satisfied with dog food when he might be able to get his jaws around a piece of steak again?

Quinn walked quickly through her parents' front yard and across into Harley's yard, then down the side of the house to the back garden. Horatio disappeared around the corner of the house in front of her. She hoped he wouldn't do too much damage before she caught up with him.

"Oh, aren't you cute?" A tall, dark-haired woman called out to Horatio and he stopped, looking behind him for Quinn, then advancing into Harley's yard and up onto the deck. He made a beeline for the woman, who knelt down and threw her arms around his neck.

He licked her face, and his tail wagged energetically. "Let's see what we can find for you to eat. Harley, look who's here! Who does this handsome specimen belong to?" the woman asked.

Quinn stood at the corner of the house and watched the woman lead Horatio over to where Harley was grilling steaks on the barbecue. She couldn't hear his response, but she saw him reach over to a side table and pick up a huge bone, holding it out to Horatio. Horatio took one look, abandoned the woman shamelessly, and took the bone from Harley's hand, carrying it over to the edge of the deck where he could gnaw on it to his heart's content.

Quinn's heart melted. So Harley was keeping his promise, making an effort to become friends with Horatio.

Quinn noticed half a dozen people standing around on the deck and she hesitated a moment before advancing. Then the same woman who had been so enamored of Horatio spied her and rushed over with a second woman in tow.

"You must be Quinn," she gushed. "Harley's told us *all* about you. Did he tell you about us? We're his sisters." Quinn looked from one woman to the other and realized one was the mirror image of the other. They were identical twins.

"I'm Cynthia and this is Joanne." Cynthia advanced toward Quinn, her hand outstretched. Joanne stood waiting for her turn. "You can tell us apart because I have a small birthmark here, just under my ear." She pointed to an almost invisible mark, and Quinn smiled, thinking the two women must have had fun in their teens, playing tricks on friends and family.

"Yes, I'm Quinn, and I'm the owner of that unruly sheepdog you were talking to a minute ago. He escaped from the kitchen when I tried to sneak out without him. I should take him back home before he gets into trouble."

"Oh, don't do that. We love dogs. He'll be fine. We'll help you keep an eye on him," Cynthia offered.

"I don't know if I should let him stay." Quinn hesitated, then added, "Harley doesn't really like him." She noticed the two women exchanging puzzled glances. Perhaps she should have kept quiet.

"Don't worry about Harley. We'll handle him, we always do," Joanne replied earnestly. "Now come and sit with us. We want to get acquainted. Harley's told us how wonderful you are, but we want to find out for ourselves."

"Just let me say hi to my folks and the other guests, and I'll join you in a minute." Quinn left the twins and quickly walked over to where her parents were standing talking to an elderly gentleman. "Hello Mother, hi Dad." She gave them each a kiss and shook hands with the gentleman who was her parents' neighbor from the other side. They chatted for a moment, then she made her way to where Harley was busy with the barbecue.

"Hello, Harley, you look as though you could use some help."

"Quinn, at last—I was getting worried about you. How was the trip from Victoria?"

"Long and slow. There was lots of traffic tonight. But other than that . . ." Her voice trailed off as she noticed Harley staring at her. "What's the matter? Do I have something on my face?"

"Nothing that shouldn't be there. I was just noticing how beautiful you look tonight. Is that a new hairdo?" He smiled and leaned toward her, whispering devilishly, "Don't jump, I'm going to give you a kiss. We have to make this look authentic." He bent over, and his lips brushed hers.

Quinn felt a shock as their lips touched, and she jumped back, her hand coming involuntarily to her mouth.

"Surely it's not that bad." He wagged his finger at her as if she were a naughty child. "You mustn't wipe my kiss away. If you do, I'll just have to give you another one." He laughed when she dropped her hand back to her side as if burned.

"That wasn't part of the bargain," she whispered.

"How do you think we're going to convince our families we're serious if they don't see a little affection between us? Was it really all that bad?"

"Well no, I guess not. You just caught me by surprise." If the truth were known, Quinn was wishing the kiss had lasted longer. It had been a long time since she'd felt the sort of emotion he stirred in her. But she mustn't let him see how much she'd enjoyed it.

"Come with me. I want to introduce you to my mother. She went into the kitchen a minute ago to put some bread in the oven." Harley took Quinn's hand and led her across the deck into the house. His mother was standing in front of the stove trying to figure out which knob turned on the oven.

"Mother, there's someone here I want you to meet. This is Quinn O'Connell. Quinn, may I present my mother, Cecile?"

"Quinn, Harley has told me about you. You'll never know how pleased I am he's found you. I was beginning to despair." She held out her hands and took Quinn's outstretched one warmly between them.

"Mother, don't scare her off by making me sound so hopeless. I need a little time to charm her first, before she finds out you'd given up on me." It was obvious Harley cared a great deal for his mother. He smiled affectionately as he teased her.

"I am sorry my husband could not be here to meet you, Quinn, but he had made arrangements to go on a fishing trip with friends and could not be persuaded to change his plans. Perhaps you will come with Harley to visit us in Vancouver so that he can meet you. He will be so pleased. You are very beautiful. Harley, you didn't tell me how lovely Quinn is," she scolded her son.

"I'm sorry, Mother, I'm just realizing how irresistible she is myself." He put his arm around Quinn's waist. Quinn shivered slightly. "Are you warm enough Quinn? You're shivering."

"It's probably just hunger and fatigue. I had a very busy day at the bookstore," Quinn explained, not wanting him to guess it was his touch that made her tremble.

Just then the twins came bounding through the door. "Harley, it's not fair of you to keep Quinn all to yourself," Cynthia said, pretending to pout. "Joanne and I want to visit with her, too. Shouldn't you be out on the deck keeping an eye on those steaks?" "Come with us, Quinn." They laughingly led her back outside.

"Don't go telling her any stories about me, you

two," Harley called after them. "I'll never forgive you if you scare her away."

"You don't need us to do that; you'll do it yourself with your ugly mug and terrible cooking," Cynthia teased.

"Look, the steaks are burning," Joanne hollered over her shoulder. She pointed to the barbecue, which was sending an inordinate amount of blue smoke into the air.

"Darn, I hope they're not ruined," Harley said as he rushed outside to rescue their dinner.

Even though they traded insults right and left, it was obvious Harley enjoyed playing big brother. She liked Harley's family very much. Too bad she wouldn't have an opportunity to get to know them better. When her bargain with Harley ended she'd probably never see them again. She felt a twinge of regret.

"All right you two, quit horsing around and help me get dinner on the table," Harley called to Joanne and Cynthia from the barbecue, where he was busy rescuing the steaks. "Everyone's hungry." He piled the steaks on a huge platter, then called out to everyone, "Dinner's served. Come to the table, please."

Cecile took the bread and some baked potatoes out of the oven, and Joanne got the salad and dressing out of the fridge. Cynthia busied herself directing people to their places at the table.

"Quinn, I want you here next to me," Cynthia said. "We still haven't had a chance to get to know each other. Joanne, you sit on Quinn's other side." She helped her mother to a place at Harley's right. He was seated at the head of the table and had asked Quinn's father to sit at the foot with Mrs. O'Connell next to him.

Seated between the two mothers was the elderly gentleman who had been talking to Quinn's parents earlier. He was recently widowed, and her parents had taken him under their wing. With Quinn in the middle of the other side and Harley's sisters on either side of her, there were eight at the table.

"I'd like to propose a toast." Harley stood up and raised his glass, which he had filled with wine along with everyone else's. "And I have an announcement."

Everyone stopped talking and stood up, waiting expectantly. All eyes were on Harley, including Quinn's.

"To friends and neighbors, and to families—Quinn's and mine. I'd like to welcome you here to share this special occasion."

What was he up to? Quinn glanced at her parents, who were waiting along with Harley's family. No one seemed to have any idea what he was going to say.

"I know this is very sudden but I'm pleased to announce that Quinn has consented to become my wife. I hope you'll all join me in a toast to my future bride." He turned smoothly toward Quinn, smiling all the while. "To Quinn."

Harley raised his glass amid squeals of delight from his sisters and shocked silence from Quinn, who swayed dizzily as the blood rushed to her head. How dare he pull a stunt like this! Especially in front of their families. This was definitely not part of their bargain. Of all the nerve!

Quinn smiled through gritted teeth as Harley's sisters, then her parents, came over to hug and congratulate her.

"Quinn, why didn't you tell us?" Her mother pouted, a tiny frown wrinkling her brow. "This is so sudden." Then she brightened, quivering excitedly. "Never mind; I'm very happy for you. Just think how much fun we'll have planning your wedding. I've dreamed of this moment for the longest time." She reached up and kissed her daughter on the cheek.

"Quinn, I hope you'll be very happy," her father added, holding her tightly. "Harley is a heck of a nice fellow. You couldn't have made a better choice as far as your mother and I are concerned."

"Thanks, Dad." *I'm going to kill Harley when this night's over,* Quinn thought, trying to stay calm as she accepted everyone's best wishes.

"Quinn, imagine, we'll be sisters," Cynthia crowed. "For the longest time Joanne and I thought Harley would never remarry. After Felicity, he was so heart-broken, we—" Cynthia broke off as she noticed the shocked look on Quinn's face. "Don't tell me Harley hasn't told you about Felicity? Uh-oh, have I put my foot in it again? I'm always getting into trouble. Rescue me, Joanne." She turned to her twin with a look of panic. "I think I've made a very big faux pas."

"I have a feeling there are a few things your brother hasn't told me," Quinn said quietly, and it would have been obvious to anyone who knew her well just how angry Quinn was, by the low tone of voice she was using. But Cynthia didn't have the benefit of experience.

"I'm sorry, I just thought . . ." Cynthia looked at Quinn as though wishing she'd never opened her mouth. Her eyes darted around the room searching for someone to help her out of her predicament. Just then

Harley happened to glance over and see his sisters crowded around Quinn, and Quinn looking as though she were ready to collapse or kill someone. He strode purposefully to her side.

"Quinn, come with me for a moment, will you? Excuse us, girls, I have something I want to show Quinn. Why don't you get everyone back to the table and go ahead with dinner? We'll be right back."

Harley led Quinn out of the dining room, through the living room, and down the hall to his study. He closed the door carefully and turned to face her.

"What's the matter, Quinn? You look pale. Is it hunger or is something else bothering you?"

Quinn was having a hard time reading Harley's expression. She wondered if he was mocking her or genuinely concerned. After all, how could a man who could be so thoughtful and solicitous not know what was upsetting her?

"You've got a darned nerve asking me that," Quinn declared. "First you announce to everyone that we're engaged, and then I find out you've been married before—just a minor detail you neglected to mention." Quinn's eyes flashed as she confronted him.

"I'm sorry." Harley paced the room. His expression was sheepish. "About the engagement thing, I honestly don't know *what* came over me. Everyone seemed so pleased about us. I just wanted to make them happy. I guess I got carried away. It was stupid of me, and I'm sorry. I'll go right out there and tell everyone it was all a big mistake if that's what you want," he finished in a contrite tone.

"What about Felicity?" Quinn challenged. "Why

didn't you tell me you'd been married before? Are you divorced?"

"I thought you knew. I'm sure I mentioned my marriage to your mother. I thought she might have told you. I shouldn't have assumed she would have said anything, I guess. Let me explain."

He led Quinn to a chair and she sat on the edge of it, not allowing herself to become comfortable. She wasn't ready to forgive him, not yet.

"It's still hard for me to talk about it," Harley explained. "I'm not divorced. Felicity and I were married in 1982. We were very much in love. We had five wonderful years together before she was killed in an automobile accident. I've been alone ever since. It's been over ten years.

"You see, I had made up my mind not to become emotionally involved with anyone ever again because I didn't want to have to go through the pain and heartbreak of losing someone I love. My family has been urging me to remarry. As I told you, my mother and sisters have been behaving just like your mother. They keep introducing women to me, hoping I'll meet that someone special and fall in love. When I met you and saw your mother putting you through the same ordeal, I thought we could help each other out. I didn't mean to mislead you. If you want to cancel our agreement, I'll tell everyone the engagement is off. But let them have this one night. It would be terribly upsetting for everyone if we went out there and told them we'd changed our minds."

Harley gave Quinn such a mournful, beseeching look that she couldn't refuse his request. Besides, she didn't really want to. It had been a shock to hear Harley tell everyone they were engaged, but now that she'd had time to adjust to the notion, in some perverse way, she kind of liked the idea.

"Well, at least we agree on that much. Whatever we decide, we'll leave things as they are for tonight. I need time to think. We'll talk about this again over the weekend," she said sternly, "but right now, I'm starving, and if I don't get something to eat, you'll have to pick me up off the floor and carry me home." With that, she got up and walked out of the study, leaving Harley behind.

On her way back to the dining room, she stopped in the bathroom to splash some water on her face and run her fingers through her hair. She had been on an emotional roller coaster, and the effect showed in her appearance. Her face was flushed, her hair disheveled and unruly. The emotional upheaval of this night would catch up with her, but right now she had to paste a big smile on her face and go back to the dining room looking as though she was the happiest woman alive, happily engaged to Harley Donaldson.

If only the engagement was real, she wouldn't have to pretend. She was beginning to realize that what she felt for Harley, in spite of the fact that he was the most infuriating man she'd ever met, was more than mere physical attraction. Quinn never wanted this night to end because when it did, they would no longer be engaged. Perhaps they would never go out again. She felt shocked and dismayed to discover she was willing to put up with Harley's little game just so she could be near him. What a colossal mess she had gotten herself into!

Chapter Six

When Quinn woke up the next morning, the memory of the events of the previous night came crowding into her head. Her spirits fell. First, there was the bargain with Harley. Then there was his big announcement of their engagement. She dreaded getting up and going into the kitchen where her mother would be itching to hear all the details of her romance and anxious to start planning a big wedding. In fact, her mother had probably called all the family and hired a caterer already. She was always so efficient and organized. Planning the wedding was just the sort of challenge she would relish. Quinn didn't think she could face the day.

She lay in bed feeling glum and sorry for herself until she heard her mother calling her from the kitchen.

"Quinn, Harley's on the phone. Pick it up in my room."

With trepidation, Quinn slipped out of bed and went down the hall to her parents' room.

"Hello."

"Good morning, Quinn. How are you feeling?"

"How do you expect me to be feeling?" Quinn grumbled, though if she were honest she would have to admit that her spirits were beginning to rise just from hearing the sound of his voice. "You've put me in a very awkward position, Harley Donaldson. Do you have any idea what you've done?"

"I'm sorry, Quinn, truly I am, but you know, I've been thinking things over, and I can't, for the life of me, see how our situation has really changed. We agreed to date. The only difference is that people think we're engaged. Both sets of parents are delighted," he explained logically. "Neither of us will have to worry about being pestered about marriage for a very long time. So where's the harm?" he finished, his tone indicating he couldn't quite understand Quinn's bad-humored response.

"Harley, you've met my mother," Quinn explained tersely. "You know what she's like. How are we going to keep her from rushing out shopping for wedding invitations and sending them out? Before we know what's hit us, we'll find ourselves married and on our way to a honeymoon in Hawaii," she concluded morosely.

"Hmm, I'm looking forward to that." Harley chuckled wickedly.

"You're not taking our predicament seriously," Quinn snapped. "What are we going to do?" She felt anger rising dangerously inside her and took a couple of deep breaths.

"Listen, Quinn," Harley replied, his voice slow and steady in direct contrast to Quinn's. "Have your shower and breakfast. I'll be over to pick you up in half an hour. Tell your mother I'm taking you shopping for a ring. While we're out we can talk over the situation and figure out what to do. I still think you're blowing this out of proportion. It's not as if we're really engaged," he concluded in an irritatingly logical tone.

That's just it, Quinn thought, her spirits sinking once again. *The whole arrangement is a farce, which would be fine if I didn't find myself wanting the real thing. What's gotten into me?* She hung up the phone and went to shower and dress. When she was ready, she went to the kitchen to face her parents. They were seated at the kitchen table, lingering over their morning coffee.

"Good morning, Mother, Dad."

"Quinn, I'm so excited!" her mother gushed, hardly allowing her time to get a coffee and sit down before she started in. "When I met Harley, I just knew he was the man for you. I'm so happy for you both. Let's you and I plan a trip to Vancouver soon so we can shop for a wedding dress."

"Hold on a minute, Mother. Let's not rush things more than they have been already. The whole idea of marriage is new to me, and I need time to get used to it. Harley and I aren't in any hurry. We need to get to know each other better before we set a date for the wedding. And when we do marry, I won't be going in for a long white dress," Quinn added firmly, knowing she had to nip her mother's enthusiasm in the bud. "I'd probably trip over the train on my way up the aisle and fall flat on my face. A simple suit or something less formal might be more appropriate."

Her mother looked disappointed, but recovered quickly and continued to chatter almost as though she hadn't heard what Quinn had said.

What am I saying? Quinn thought. *Anyone would think I was really going to marry Harley Donaldson.* Then she remembered he had said he was coming over in half an hour. "Harley's on his way over. He said something about going shopping for a ring."

Marjorie positively squealed with delight, and for just a moment, Quinn felt wistful. Her mother hadn't been this happy with her in years. Too bad this fiasco was going to end in disappointment.

"Your mother and I are very happy for you Quinn, but are you sure this is what you want?" her father asked when he could get a word in edgewise. "It's happened very suddenly. We want to be sure you're happy, too."

"Yes, Dad, it's what I want," Quinn replied quietly. At least that much was true; she wouldn't have wanted to lie to her father.

The doorbell rang and Marjorie went rushing to the door to let Harley in. "Good morning, Harley. Let me give you a hug. Robert and I are so happy for you and Quinn. Come in and have a cup of coffee." She reached up, standing on her tiptoes, and threw her arms around Harley.

"Good morning, Marjorie. I think I'll pass on the coffee, if you don't mind. Quinn and I have a very special errand to run." He winked at her and she got all flustered. "We'd best be going. Quinn, are you ready?" Harley was dressed in faded jeans and a casual green corduroy shirt and looked relaxed and happy.

Quinn drained her coffee mug and went to get a sweater. She didn't say anything to Harley until they were driving down the street, well away from her parents' house. "I hope you've had time to come up with a solution to our little dilemma, Harley. You should have heard my mother this morning. She was already planning a shopping excursion to Vancouver to go hunting for a wedding dress."

"Really?" Harley kept his eyes on the road, but considered what Quinn had said and responded seriously, "Actually, I see you in a cream-colored silk suit rather than a formal wedding gown. I don't think that's your style." He smiled at her, turning his reply into a joke while making her heart jump erratically.

"Harley, you're not taking this seriously. What are we going to do?" Quinn's tone leaned toward desperation.

Finally Harley paid attention. He turned off the busy road they were travelling onto a quiet side street, pulled over, and turned off the motor. Turning to Quinn, he put his hand under her chin, tilting her face toward him. He bent down and kissed her lips, then the tip of her nose.

Quinn melted like an ice cube in the hot sun. For a moment, she almost believed he cared. But before she could dissolve in his arms and return the kiss, she made herself pull away.

"What do you think you're doing? I thought we were supposed to be coming up with a graceful way out of our phony engagement!" she said, trying to hide her true feelings in a show of anger.

"I *have* been thinking, Quinn, and here's what I've come up with. I think we should go shopping for a ring just like we told your mother we planned to do. Then we'll tell our families we want to take a few months to get to know each other better before setting a date for the wedding. Some time over the course of the next few months, we'll tell them we've decided the engagement was a mistake. How about that?"

"I don't know." Quinn hesitated.

"We can't just call the engagement off right away. We'd have to tell them the whole thing was a hoax. That would make us pretty unpopular. This way, they'll leave us alone for the time being, as we intended. Like I said on the phone, nothing has really changed," Harley concluded.

"Well, when you put it like that, I suppose you're right. But somehow, saying we're engaged seems so much more permanent than just telling our folks we're dating."

"Don't worry, I don't intend to hold you to it. As far as I'm concerned, this is an engagement of convenience, nothing more," he said smoothly.

He sought to reassure her but his words had the opposite effect. Quinn's heart sank. She knew he was absolutely right, but deep down, she'd almost begun to believe the engagement was for real. It still hurt that he seemed to be able to carry this charade off so matter-of-factly, while she was suffering inside. Well, she certainly wouldn't let him know that.

"Very well. If you can manage it, I'm sure I can. It doesn't matter to me one way or the other. Just so long as you know it's strictly business," Quinn asserted, trying to be nonchalant.

"Right."

Did Harley's voice sound more gruff than usual? Perhaps it was just wishful thinking on Quinn's part, but for a moment, she thought she saw a look of regret cross his face. Then he adopted a bland expression as he spoke again.

"Now, let's go shopping," he said matter-of-factly.

Harley drove downtown where the malls were about to open. Parking well away from the crowded area, they walked to the entrance and he led Quinn to an exclusive jewelry store. Leaving her to admire the showcase, he conferred with the proprietor, who went into a back room and returned with a black velvet case. He ushered Quinn and Harley to the reception area, pulling out a chair for Quinn in front of a small display table.

"Now, I think you'll be pleased with what I have to show you, sir. This ring is quite perfect for the lady, with her coloring." He opened the case, and Quinn gasped in awe.

"Slip it on, madam, I think it may be just the right size for you." He held out the ring, a huge rectangular-cut emerald set in gold, with a halo of tiny diamonds around it. The ring was simple yet elegant, and obviously very expensive.

"Harley, this is too much," Quinn protested.

"Let me be the judge of that." Harley dismissed her comment with a wave of his hand. "I think the gentleman is right. The ring, with that emerald, is perfect for someone with your coloring." He picked up the ring and, taking hold of Quinn's left hand, slipped it on her third finger. It slid over her knuckle snugly, but once in place, fit perfectly. Even though the emerald was large, Quinn's hand could handle it, her fingers being long and sturdy. She mentally thanked Dani for having insisted she have a manicure, since the ring drew attention to her hands.

The salesman turned on a small table lamp, and as Quinn moved her hand, turning it this way and that, the precious jewels caught the light and sparkled brilliantly. She turned back to Harley, trying once again to make him see reason.

"Don't you think this is a little extravagant, given the circumstances?"

"The circumstances are that I have just become engaged and that I love to buy beautiful things for my fiancée. The ring is perfect on your hand. It looks as though it were made for you," he said firmly, ignoring her protests. "If you like it, we'll take it." He looked questioningly at Quinn.

"Of course I like it, who wouldn't?"

"Then, that's settled." He got up abruptly, turning to the salesman. "Don't bother to wrap it. The lady will wear it home."

The salesman grinned broadly, obviously thinking of his commission, which would be considerable. "of course, sir. A wise choice, if I may say so."

Harley went to arrange payment while Quinn sat gazing at the ring in amazement. This was silly of Harley. After all, what was he going to do with the ring when their engagement ended? Quinn mused. Perhaps save it for a real fiancée? She felt a terrible pain sweep through her at the thought of someone else being engaged to Harley and wearing her ring. She banished the thought, and that's when she decided to enjoy herself and savor every moment of their engagement. It wouldn't last forever, and when it ended, all that would remain would be her memories. And if the pain she felt just thinking about the inevitable end was any indication, life after Harley would be grim.

"Come on, Quinn," Harley interjected, snapping her back from her somber thoughts. "I'll take you home. My mother and sisters are leaving this afternoon. I'd like you to come over for dinner tonight, just you and me. What do you say? I think it's time we got to know each other better." He bent down and kissed her lightly on the lips, then took a firm hold of her hand and led her back to the car.

Quinn noticed that Harley seemed to be getting freer with his affections, both private and public. It had the effect of keeping her guessing and off balance.

"Whatever you say, Harley," she said, breathless from his touch. Then she mentally kicked herself for sounding like such a pushover. What was happening to her? She had never been like this with any man before. Their engagement was supposed to be a fake; why did she keep on forgetting?

Harley opened the passenger door of the Mercedes and Quinn slid onto the cool leather seat. Not trusting herself to be able to conceal her feelings if she spoke, she sat silently while he drove. Soon he was pulling up in front of her parents' house. Horatio barked when the car pulled up, then came dashing out to greet them, crushing a few of her mother's flowers on the way.

"What time is dinner, Harley?" Quinn asked as she got out and shut the car door.

"Any time after seven."

"Okay, I'll see you later." Quinn turned to walk toward the house. "Horatio, don't walk on the flowers, or Mother will give you cat food for supper," Quinn tried to joke with Horatio, but he just looked up at her, his head cocked to one side. She laughed at his puzzled expression. Sometimes she had the feeling he understood every word she said. "Come on, silly." She reached down to scratch his nose affectionately. "Let's go."

Quinn turned and waved at Harley as he moved the car ahead and drove into his driveway. Squaring her shoulders, she readied herself to face her mother's questions, then walked briskly down the sidewalk to the door.

Before she could use her key, her mother flung open the door, took one look at Quinn's left hand, and exclaimed in a voice that seemed much too loud for her small size, "Quinn, my heavens, look at that! Howard, come and see Quinn's ring." She turned back to Quinn and said seriously, in a tone that made Quinn chuckle in spite of herself, "You are a very lucky woman, Quinn. That Harley is such a gentleman, and a rich one at that. Now come inside and let's talk weddings."

As Quinn lay flat out in the bathtub later that evening, she felt a thrill of anticipation. She was going to dine with Harley—in his house—alone. Was she ready for this? If not now, then never. She had given up trying to talk herself out of the growing attraction she felt for him. She was no longer pretending, fooling herself into thinking that her plan to break his heart was on track. There had been a serious derailment. She wasn't quite sure how or when it had started to go

wrong, but she knew she was in this phony engagement up to her eyeballs. She had decided to play it for
all it was worth and to heck with the consequences.

She slowly let the water run out of the bathtub as
she stood up to dry off, rubbing her skin gently with
the thick, soft towel. Then she dressed in some of the
new clothes Dani had helped her choose.

The sundress she and Dani had chosen was a pretty
cotton print, with several shades of blue from navy to
turquoise, thrown together in a splash of swirls, like
an abstract canvas. The top was low, and the skirt
short. In fact, she remembered complaining that, considering the amount of material used to make it, the
dress must be made of spun gold, since the price was
outrageously high. Dani had dismissed her complaints
and insisted she buy it. And examining herself in the
mirror, she knew Dani had been right. She looked
good. If this dress didn't knock him down a peg or
two, nothing would.

Quinn applied just a touch of makeup, as the woman
at the salon had demonstrated, and was pleasantly surprised at the effect. Her features looked soft and
dreamy. A little perfume dabbed behind her ears and
she was ready to beard the lion in his den. She went
into the living room to say good-bye to her parents.

"Quinn, you look like an apparition tonight," her
father commented.

"Thanks, Dad. I feel like one. The speed at which
events of the last couple of days have taken place has
knocked the wind out of my sails. I should be staying
home and going to bed early, but here I am going to
dinner with a strange man, who just happens to be my
fiancée. Will wonders never cease?" She laughed, hop-

ing her father wouldn't catch the nervousness in her voice.

"Now don't stay out too late, young lady," he admonished laughingly. "I don't want to have to come looking for you."

"Don't wait up, Dad. Harley and I have lots of things to discuss. I may be late." She bent over to give him a kiss.

"Just make sure you have a good time."

"I plan to," Quinn replied.

At that moment Quinn's mother came in from the kitchen, looking Quinn over with a critical eye.

"That dress seems a little short, Quinn. But you look quite pretty," she conceded, almost as an afterthought.

Quinn grimaced but decided determinedly not to let her mother spoil her mood. "This length is what all the best-dressed women are wearing this season, Mother," she joked. "I'd better go; I don't want to be late. Will you feed Horatio for me? I almost forgot."

Quinn walked quickly into the kitchen to say goodbye to him and he looked up from his mat with a pathetically sad expression. At least it seemed sad, though his eyes were not visible through his shaggy bangs.

"Don't try to make me feel bad, Horatio. You have to stay home tonight. I don't want you to witness your mistress making a big fool of herself." With that, Quinn gave Horatio a quick kiss on the nose and let herself out the door.

It was a beautifully warm evening and the sun was still visible just above the horizon. Its dying rays sent shafts of color through the sky, bright pinks and oranges that changed constantly as it sank lower. This hour of the evening was Quinn's favorite time of day. She stopped to admire the sky for a moment before crossing into Harley's yard and going up the sidewalk to the front door.

He must have been waiting just inside the door, because it opened as soon as she rang the doorbell.

"Quinn, you look wonderful," he exclaimed. He took her hands and pulled her inside. "May I give my fiancée a kiss?" Without waiting for her answer, he bent his head and kissed her deeply.

Quinn reeled dizzily. What kind of game was he playing? He acted as though kissing her was as natural to him as breathing. If she didn't know better she would think he really cared.

"Come on through and we'll sit outside for a little while, while it's still warm. We can watch the sunset." He took her hand and led her through the living room into the kitchen and out through the sliding glass doors to the lounger on the deck. "What can I get you to drink?"

"How about a glass of seltzer water?"

"All right, sit down and admire the view while I open the bottle."

Quinn looked out over the backyard and beyond. The night before when she had arrived for the barbecue, it had been too dark to see the spectacular view from Harley's deck. The yard faced a grassy area, which was part of the Middle Island Golf and Country Club. It was gently sloped and spread out toward the ocean. While the property was not on the waterfront, the elevation was high enough that she had an unobstructed view of the strait and beyond it some of the smaller islands that made up the Gulf Islands.

"Here you are." Harley handed Quinn a glass. "I want to propose a toast. To our engagement—may it be long and mutually satisfying." He smiled wickedly. Quinn wondered what surprises he had up his sleeve tonight.

"To our engagement," Quinn said, puzzling over his choice of words. She let it pass. "Do you need help with dinner?"

"No thanks. Your mother's told me how much you hate cooking, so I think I'll let you sit and enjoy yourself while I put the finishing touches on our meal. I hope you like chicken? I have some on the barbecue."

"My mother certainly hasn't left me many secrets, has she? Well, at least you know what kind of bargain you're getting. I don't cook and I don't clean," she joked, pretending the engagement was for real and that they would marry one day.

"I would never expect you to," he parried, going along with her little game. "A busy career woman like you has much more important things to do. Tell me all about your business. The bookstore looks as though it does well. Whenever I stop in, the store is bustling with people. Do you enjoy it?"

"I love it and would never want to give it up."

She told him about how she had hunted for just the right business before she had invested and how she'd built it up over the past three years. "Lately, I've been a little worried, though. There's a new bookstore in Victoria, one of those warehouse operations. Many of the smaller stores like mine have been losing business. I don't know what I'm going to do. You haven't met Dani, the woman who works for me; she's a very good friend as well as an employee. I fear if the trend continues, I may have to cut her hours back."

"I've seen her when I've been in the store. That's unfortunate. Isn't there something else you can do?"

"If you have any suggestions, I'm all ears. I've wracked my brain and haven't come up with any ideas to bring more business to the store. We've tried all the usual things: advertising, promotions, sales. We've even held book-signings, but people don't come out to see unknown authors; it has to be someone big and famous. And the famous writers don't come to tiny bookstores like mine. I guess they think they won't sell enough books." Quinn took a sip of her wine before looking up at Harley.

"I have an idea," Harley said thoughtfully. "What if I told you I could get Herbert Davis to come to the store to promote his new book? You know, the one you accidentally tried to sell me the other day?" He reminded her of the slip she'd made. "Do you think people would come out to see him?"

"Are you kidding? Of course they would. He's really hot right now. But how could you possibly do that? You don't even read his books. In fact you were quite disturbed about being offered *The Happy Captive* even by mistake. Don't tease, Harley, it's a serious problem for Dani and me."

Quinn was tense. The evening wasn't going at all the way she'd planned. She had hoped Harley's invitation would set the stage for a very special night. She hadn't thought they would end up talking about her business problems.

"I'm not teasing you," Harley regarded her earnestly. "I'm dead serious. Just because I don't read the man's books, doesn't mean I can't deliver. Trust me. If I say I can get him to your store to sign copies of his book, then I can. Don't you believe me?" He looked insulted, turning away to pour himself another glass of wine.

"If you say so, then I guess I believe you," she said doubtfully. "After all, what reason could you have to play such a mean trick? Unless, of course, you're still trying to get even for that steak Horatio stole." A smile twitched on her lips as she recalled the event. "If you could somehow manage to arrange for him to come to the store to meet my customers and sign his books, I would be forever in your debt. If Herbert Davis made a personal appearance at the bookstore, it just might help turn things around. A lot of women would come to see him, and once they were there and saw what the store had to offer, they'd be sure to come back. But . . ." She hesitated. "I've heard he never does personal appearances; he's a bit of a hermit. What makes you think you can get him to agree to do this? Is he a friend of yours?"

"Quinn, do you trust me or not?" Harley asked impatiently. "What kind of marriage are we going to have if you can't trust me to keep my word?" He tossed the word "marriage" into the conversation as if it belonged there, yet to Quinn it felt as though he'd thrown a live grenade. She couldn't decided whether to ignore it and hope it would go away or lob it back to him and let him deal with it. She decided to ignore it, because she was struggling to keep the conversation light. She wanted to continue probing his possible acquaintance with Davis instead of taking up his challenge.

"How and when do you propose to get Davis to come to the store?" she asked.

"Leave the *how* to me. I'm not going to give away all my secrets, even to you. As for the *when,* that's up to you. Just name the date, and I'll make the arrangements. But be sure you have lots of his books on hand. I've heard that on the rare occasions he does make an appearance, it's a real mob scene."

"Okay." Now Quinn was starting to get excited. She stood up and began pacing up and down the deck, thinking out loud. "I'll have to order lots of extra stock. I think I could be ready in three to four weeks." Then she turned back to Harley, her eyes shining. "Let me talk to Dani and I'll get back to you with a date. This is wonderful, the best news I've had in weeks." She clapped her hands together in glee. "Now, where's that supper you've been promising me? I'm starving."

"Oh, how I love a lady with a good appetite! Step right this way, please." Harley bowed slightly and pointed to the table in his best maître d' style. He led Quinn back into the house, to the dining room. The room looked quite different than the night before. The table had been made smaller and set with fine linen and china. There was a low flower arrangement made up of colorful spring blossoms and greenery as a centrepiece. Harley lit candles on either side of the arrangement and turned the lights down low, creating an intimate setting, one of romance.

This was what Quinn had been expecting when she'd prepared for the evening, yet all of a sudden she felt strangely shy. She'd always been outgoing and sociable and comfortable in any situation. Yet as she looked up at Harley, she felt suddenly ill at ease and tenuous as if she'd never been alone with a man before. Why did he have this overwhelming effect on her?

"Better turn up the lights; I'm liable to eat the flowers by mistake," she joked feebly, trying to diffuse some of the energy in the room and relieve the tension.

"Relax, Quinn, I'm not going to bite you." Harley laughed. "Though you *do* look good enough to eat. Did I mention how beautiful you are tonight? You take my breath away."

"Thank you, Harley," Quinn replied, trying to think of a snappy rejoinder, but coming up short.

He pulled out her chair and she sat down. He left her alone for a moment while he went to bring the chicken in from the barbecue, then looked for the salad from the fridge and a rice dish he had put in the oven to keep warm. As she watched him bustle about the kitchen, she was impressed. He was a man of many talents, not the least of which was making her heart beat faster.

"Okay, I think we're ready. We'll start with some pâté and fresh bread. My mother is French and she has instilled in me a love of good food." He cut a slice of bread for Quinn and passed it to her, along with a small slice of pâté nestled on a bed of lettuce and surrounded by tiny, tart pickles.

"I thought I detected a slight accent. Is she from Quebec? How did she and your father meet?"

"Actually she's originally from Paris. They met in France when he was working there in the Canadian Embassy. They were married in France, and when he was transferred back to Canada, she emigrated. She's lost most of her accent over the years. One hardly notices it except when she becomes excited or upset."

Dinner was long and leisurely, and Quinn enjoyed the easy flow of the conversation. Harley was witty and interesting and had no trouble keeping her attention. In fact, she couldn't take her eyes off him, and he behaved as though he felt the same way. The flickering candles cast a romantic glow, heightening the romantic ambience. It was late when they finally got up from the table and went to sit in the living room.

Quinn excused herself for a moment and went to the washroom. On her way back to the living room, as she walked down the hall she noticed the door into Harley's study was open, so she peeked inside. There was a large oak desk with a small notebook computer sitting on it. One wall was covered with bookshelves, which were crowded with books. Quinn itched to get a look at them. She had always felt one could learn a lot about a person by the books he read. As she looked inside the room, she noticed Harley watching her from the living room. Reluctantly, she turned away and made her way down the hall to rejoin him.

As Quinn went to sit in a comfortable chair near the fireplace, Harley, who was standing in the center of the room, took hold of her hands and pulled her toward him. When she moved forward, she caught her foot in the carpet and fell against his broad chest.

"Are you okay? Did you hurt yourself?" He looked down at her with concern.

"I'm fine. I just caught my heel. I'm not used to these blasted things." With an air of impatience, she reached down and slipped off her shoes. "There, that's better."

He put his hand under her elbow to steady her, then as she stood up, gathered her into his arms. "I've been telling myself all evening that it's not a good idea for us to get involved. This is not part of our bargain. But I can't help it; you drive me crazy, Quinn." He bent his head and kissed her, holding her tightly against his chest.

Quinn's lips parted as she accepted his kiss eagerly, then when it ended, she looked up at him, smiling shyly. "Well, you have that effect on me too, but I don't think it's a good idea for us to give in to our feelings. It's too soon, and besides, remember this is not a real relationship, it's pretend." Even as she reminded him of the temporary nature of their relationship, she reached up and kissed him full on the lips. He returned the kiss, and then reluctantly held her at arm's length.

"Hey, maybe this engagement wasn't such a great idea after all," he mumbled, his voice thick. "I'm not sure I can keep my distance. But I'll try," he added sheepishly.

Quinn, too, felt dizzy, but she knew she had to rein in her feelings lest she be swept away by the moment. She knew she would regret it if she didn't. She reached up to put her hand on his cheek.

"Come on, let's sit down. We can talk a little before I go home."

Chapter Seven

Quinn sat up suddenly, looking around her in panic. For a moment she didn't remember where she was, but then she made out the shadowy dining room where she and Harley had shared a leisurely dinner a few hours before.

She held up her wrist so she could see her watch. 3:30 A.M. She hadn't meant to fall asleep after dinner, but the stress of the past few days must have caught up with her. She remembered snuggling with Harley on the sofa. They had talked about this and that, making an effort to avoid the issue of their feelings for each other. She remembered yawning and curling up in his arms. After that, it was all a huge blank. She must have dozed off. How embarrassing!

Quinn realized she felt warm and toasty all over She looked down to see a warm quilt tucked around her. A fluffy feather pillow cushioned her head. Harley must have covered her before heading for his own bed. She sank back down onto the comfortable sofa, and closed her eyes once again. Just a few more minutes and she'd get up and make her escape before he wakened.

She wanted to be home before her parents got up. It would be embarrassing to arrive in the morning and have to listen to her mother's comments and see her inquisitive glances.

The next thing Quinn knew, Harley was standing over her with a steaming cup of coffee.

"Quinn, it's six o'clock. If you want to be back home before your parents wake up you'd better get up now. Here, have some coffee." He held out the mug, which she took gratefully. Then he sat on the edge of the sofa beside her as she drank it. She propped herself up on one elbow, holding the quilt around her, feeling a little out of sorts and embarrassed for having fallen asleep on Harley's couch.

"You have no secrets from me now, Quinn O'Connell," Harley joked. "I've even heard you snoring," he teased.

Oh, yes I do, Quinn thought. *You don't know that I love you. And I'm going to do my best to make sure you never find out.*

"I don't snore!" Quinn wasn't in the mood for jokes.

Harley guffawed. "Drink up your coffee, then you'd better be off if you don't want to encounter your parents at the breakfast table." He smiled.

"You're right." She turned to him shyly. "I had a wonderful time last night, Harley. Good-bye." She headed for the door.

"Not so fast. Give me a kiss before you go." He lowered his head and kissed her deeply, releasing her reluctantly. "I suppose you're heading back to Victoria today? I'll call you."

Quinn wished there was a way to get from Harley's to her parents' without going through the front yard, but there wasn't. It would be embarrassing to be seen by one of the neighbors. She walked quickly down the sidewalk and into her parents' yard, then opened the door into the kitchen as quietly as possible. Just as she shut the door she heard footsteps coming toward the kitchen.

"Quinn, you're up already." Her mother came into the room. "I didn't hear you come in last night. Horatio woke me up just now. I thought I heard him bark at something."

Thank goodness! She thinks I've been here all along, Quinn thought. *I'm not going to disillusion her.*

"Good morning, Mother."

"I'm going back to bed for a little while. You can look after Horatio," her mother said and turned to go back through the living room to her bedroom. Quinn heaved a huge sigh of relief. Now that she'd had a cup of coffee, she was wide awake. She decided to stay up, get changed, and take Horatio for a walk.

She went to her room, took off her dress, and pulled on a pair of jeans and flannel shirt. Then she found her running shoes and carried them back to the kitchen.

When Horatio saw the shoes in Quinn's hand he danced around the kitchen, jumping up and racing in circles by the door. She grabbed his leash and hustled him out of the house before he could wake up her father.

A trail ran from the corner of her parents' property down past the far reaches of the golf course, winding its way through a forested area to the water's edge. This was the path that Quinn took with Horatio. He bounded ahead of her, full of energy, stopping to sniff here and there, and generally behaving like an over-grown puppy.

Quinn trailed dreamily behind him, still feeling the effects of her evening with Harley. She had gotten herself into a pretty pickle. She had gone and fallen in love with him, while he was merely having a good time, totally oblivious of her feelings. From the first time she'd seen him, she'd been afraid something like this would happen. Why was it her lot in life to always fall for the wrong sort of man? The ones she chose were either totally unsuitable or uninterested in any-thing serious; they wanted no strings attached. Harley fell into the latter category.

If she had any sense, she would end her bargain with Harley right away, before things went any fur-ther. As soon as she had this thought, she dismissed it. She couldn't bear the thought of never feeling his strong arms around her again. She was hooked, no doubt about it. She didn't want to do anything rash that might put an end to them being together.

She looked at the beautiful ring on her finger. Until Harley got tired of her or their bargain, she was his. But he must never know how she felt. She didn't want him to feel obligated to her, nor did she want to scare him away. For the time being, she would pretend to be having a lighthearted relationship, just like him.

To complicate matters, she and Harley had to convince others they were in love and preparing to marry. *"Oh, what a tangled web we weave,"* she thought.

Quinn thought about Harley's offer to get Herbert Davis to do a book-signing at the bookstore. That was a puzzle. How did he know Davis? And why was he so sure he could convince him to make a public appearance? Not that she would question him too closely; it could be just what the store needed. She started to get excited again, just thinking about it. She'd better head back to Victoria and get started on putting together the book order she needed to prepare for his appearance. She wanted to talk to Dani, too. Dani had lots of good ideas when it came to organizing events. They would spruce up the store, set up some special displays, arrange for a caterer. So much to do.

"Come on, Horatio, let's go," she called to the dog, who was ahead of her on the trail. He stopped and turned to look at her, then reluctantly trotted back to her side. "Let's go, fella. We've got a long day ahead of us."

"Quinn, where did you get that rock?" Dani squealed as Quinn held out her hand to show her the engagement ring Harley had given her.

Quinn, who had decided to say nothing until Dani noticed the ring, hadn't had long to wait. The next morning she was barely in the store and reaching for her first coffee of the day when Dani spotted the ring and pointed to it, her mouth agape.

"From Harley, of course. Remember our little shopping excursions? Well, you performed miracles, Dani, old girl. Your plan worked!"

"I've never seen such a beautiful ring. Is that an emerald?"

"It is. Have you ever seen anything so beautiful?" Quinn grinned happily, unconsciously echoing Dani.

"You have to tell me everything."

"Not everything," Quinn protested, with a wicked grin on her face. Then the grin disappeared as she thought about her situation. "Oh, Dani, I'm in a real mess. I'm engaged all right, but it's a farce. Harley still thinks we're playing a trick on our families. He doesn't really want to marry me. I wish I could be as blasé about this as he is but unfortunately I'm not made like that. I've gone and fallen in love." She moaned.

"But that's wonderful." Dani crossed the store and gave Quinn a big hug.

"No, it's not," Quinn protested. "I'm going to end up with a broken heart. I should put a stop to it right now, but I don't want to, because then he'll disappear out of my life and I'll be left with nothing."

"Nonsense. Don't be such a big baby. Where's your spirit of adventure?" Dani scolded. "You'll have just what you had before he came along—your career, your friends and family, and Horatio. Don't go getting all melodramatic, Quinn. You have to approach this whole situation with an open mind. Maybe Harley will fall in love with you too," Dani said hopefully. "Maybe he already has. But if he hasn't and the relationship ends at some point, at least you'll have had fun in the meantime. You've got to learn to take chances, Quinn."

"And I thought you were a romantic. You're being so cold and practical."

"That's easy, 'cuz it's your heart that's going to be broken, not mine!" Dani joked. "Just kidding!" she added hastily. "If you want to know what I think, I think he's already in love with you. What guy in his right mind would announce his engagement to someone in front of so many witnesses unless he meant it? What we have to do is plan a strategy to make sure that if I'm wrong and he isn't in love, he will fall head over heels. I can't let you blow this. He's the first guy in years who's been able to get you even mildly interested."

"Good idea, but we're going to have to put my love life on the back burner for now. I have something even more exciting to tell you." Quinn proceeded to tell Dani all about the book-signing Harley was arranging, explaining that she'd been looking for a way to encourage more business.

"I'm relieved. I know things have been slowing down since The Warehouse opened and I was about to suggest that you cut back my hours. Not that I wanted you to, but I knew you'd be too loyal to suggest it yourself."

It was Quinn's turn to give Dani a hug. "You're such a good friend, Dani. I don't know what I'd do without you."

"Frankly, I don't know either," Dani teased. "Now let's get to work; we've got lots to do before the big day."

They decided on Friday, June 13 for the event. It was only three weeks away. Quinn called Harley to let him know. The conversation was brief and imper-

sonal and Quinn's feelings were hurt when he didn't
refer to the evening they'd spent together. When she
suggested the thirteenth, he merely repeated the date
absentmindedly, said he would check with Davis and
call her back, then hung up. When he called to confirm, Quinn was out of the store on an errand, and
Dani took the call. He told her the date was fine with
Davis, suggested they make it an evening engagement
and serve wine and cheese, then rang off, not mentioning Quinn at all.

Quinn and Dani had only a short time to prepare.
During lulls between customers, they mapped out a
plan for a major cleanup of the store. They planned
where to set up a table for Davis and sorted out the
details of the food and beverages. Dani volunteered to
decorate the store and set up a special display of the
author's previous books as well as the current best-
seller, *The Happy Captive*.

Quinn decided to handle the advertising herself. She
normally kept a file of customers' names and the
books they bought, so she put together a list of names
of women she thought would be interested in coming
to the gala evening. She designed an announcement
on the computer and prepared envelopes to mail it out.
She put two announcements in each envelope, asking
each of her customers to invite a friend.

Dani made a poster for the store and as soon as it
went up, it generated lots of attention. It seemed there
would be no problem in getting a large turnout to the
store on the thirteenth.

There were a few anxious moments when the dis-
tribution company called and said they couldn't supply
all the books Quinn had ordered, but even that was

resolved quickly when Quinn called Harley to confirm last-minute details and happened to mention it. Shortly after, she had a call from the distributor, saying he had held back a few dozen books from other orders so he could supply her with the number she'd requested. It looked as though everything was working out as planned.

Quinn sang as she worked, feeling more optimistic about the store than she had in a very long time, and especially about her ability to turn things around and keep Dani working full time.

The only area of Quinn's life that wasn't going just the way she wanted was her relationship with Harley. Since their evening together, she'd hardly spoken to him, except to discuss the details of the book-signing. He had not called her. He seemed cold and distant.

Her feelings were in turmoil over his behavior. Perhaps he had thought better of their deepening involvement. She could understand why he might be feeling somewhat overwhelmed. She certainly was. Neither of them had expected to become so involved. But it hurt that what had meant so much to her, appeared to have meant little to him. She began to rethink her decision to stay in the phony engagement.

Just when she had almost made up her mind to call the whole thing off, Harley finally called. It was late in the evening and she was at home, curled up in bed with the Herbert Davis book, which she'd been trying to read for the past couple of weeks. She wanted to finish it before Davis's appearance at the store. Even though she wasn't really in the mood for love and romance, she thought it only right that she read his book so she could discuss it with him when they met.

She had just settled down with a glass of milk and some cookies when the phone rang. She answered in a distracted tone.

"Yes?"

"Quinn, how are you?" Harley's deep, husky voice sent her heart racing, but she answered warily.

"I'm fine. How are you?" *Stay calm, Quinn. Don't let him know you've been waiting for his call.*

"I'm fine. I'm sorry I haven't called, but I've been very busy this past week or so. I had a small contract for some writing and editing, and the deadline crept up on me. I had to put in some long days and nights to finish the work on time. I know I've neglected you shamelessly. I hope you're not angry with me?" he coaxed.

The negative feelings Quinn had been harboring quickly melted as she listened to Harley's explanation. She didn't want him to know she'd been hurt, so she replied casually, "That's okay, I've been really busy myself, getting the book-signing organized. I've hardly had time to notice you hadn't called."

There was a small silence on the other end of the line, then Harley responded. "I had hoped you might have missed me just a little."

Quinn didn't respond. No way she would give him the satisfaction of knowing she had waited each evening for his call and gone to bed disappointed when it hadn't come.

"I was thinking of driving into town this weekend. Can we get together?"

"When are you coming? I'll be working Saturday, but I'm free in the evening."

"How about if I pick you up around seven and we'll

go for dinner? Would you like to go to the Apollo again or try something new?"

"Let's stick with the Apollo. We're sure to have a good meal there," said Quinn, mollified that he was finally inviting her out.

"Right then, I'll see you at seven."

When Quinn got off the phone, she felt unreasonably happy. She reflected on the fact that it was silly to allow Harley to rule her moods, as well as every other aspect of her life. But she couldn't control the smile that played on her lips as she settled down again with her cookies and milk and the Herbert Davis romance.

Davis's story was set in the late 1800s in England. The heroine was a beautiful young woman, dissatisfied with her lot in life, which was that of a proper English gentlewoman. She had an independent, adventurous streak, something that was highly frowned upon in those days. She was never allowed to go out alone nor to become involved in activities considered unladylike by her family. Unhappily, almost everything she wanted to do seemed to fall into that category.

In desperation, she accepted a proposal of marriage from a neighbor, whom she knew did not love her, nor did she love him. It was a trade-off. She hoped marriage would allow her to live more independently, while he would benefit by ceasing to be the object of invitations from mothers with designs on his station and income for their marriageable daughters. He was seen as an eligible bachelor but hated the superficiality of the Victorian lifestyle.

As Quinn continued to read, she began, to her dismay, to see parallels between the book and her life. She too, was independent, desiring nothing more than to be left alone to live her life. She had entered into an engagement of convenience, one which was supposed to have allowed both her and Harley to have a break from the interference of family in their love lives. As she read on, she realized the person who benefited most from the situation in the book was the husband, who pursued his interests while his wife was left alone at home. The heroine had erred in thinking that marriage would mean freedom for her. She now found herself locked in a loveless marriage, trapped by custom into a different but equally stultifying set of social behaviors. She was even more unhappy than when she was single, if that was possible.

Quinn thought again of Harley and herself. In a way, he benefited more from their arrangement than she. She had made the mistake of falling in love with the hero of her story. The story in the book ended with the heroine being swept off her feet by her real hero, a friend of her husband's, who, in love with her himself, had noticed her unhappiness. He stormed in and took her away.

In Quinn's case, her hero was Harley. Unfortunately, she could see no happy ending to her story. Harley was enjoying his freedom. His family had stopped pestering him to remarry, and, to top it off, he was having a pleasant little dalliance with Quinn, something he seemed to be enjoying very much, without having to worry about commitment.

As Quinn read on, she realized her situation was much worse than the one faced by the heroine in the novel. She began to feel angry with Harley and with her favorite author, who, she had not noticed until this very moment, was terribly biased in favor of men. Reading the book helped her put her own situation into perspective. She realized it could not continue. The longer it went on, the harder it would be to end it and the more she would suffer when she did.

Feeling miserable, in direct contrast to the happily-ever-after ending of the book, she turned off the light and tried to sleep. She tossed and turned, finally dreaming of being swept away, into the arms of a man on horseback who looked a lot like Harley, and carried across the English countryside. Morning came far too soon.

Chapter Eight

Saturday rolled around and Quinn, working away at the store, felt nervous in anticipation of her date with Harley. She was determined to end their engagement and bow out of the bargain they'd made, yet she didn't know if she'd find the strength to follow through when Harley was actually sitting across from her. He held such an attraction for her that she seemed to melt and be incapable of rational thought in his presence. Dani thought she was crazy to even contemplate such a drastic step and didn't hesitate to make her feelings known as she and Quinn worked side by side.

"Quinn, I told you, don't give up on Harley so quickly. I'm sure things are going to work out. Wait a while before you make up your mind."

"Dani, I can't. The longer I wait the harder it will be. He doesn't have strong feelings for me. He likes me, but that's not enough compared to what I feel. I have to extricate myself from the situation while I still can."

"At least wait until after your date tonight," Dani pleaded as if she had ordered a miracle and expected it to be delivered that evening during dinner.

"I guess it won't hurt," Quinn said reluctantly, yet perversely happy she'd enjoy one more evening with Harley.

"I'm sure you won't regret it." Dani's smile lit up the store. "Now, why don't you go home early and take a nice long bubble bath. And wear that red silk dress we bought. No man, not even Harley, can resist it."

Quinn grumbled about how much work she had to do, but Dani insisted so she and Horatio left early to go home and prepare for the evening. She took Dani's advice and ran a hot bath, then soaked in the tub for ages until she felt relaxed and mellow and a little like a wrinkled prune. Then she dressed and made up her face, leaving off her dress until closer to 7:00. She put on her dressing gown and sat down with the newspaper.

Horatio lay at her feet, occasionally leaning over to lick her ankle or look up at her with a melancholy expression.

At 6:45, Quinn slipped on her dress, ran a comb through her hair, and let Horatio out for a run. She filled his water dish, then let him back in and settled him down on his mat. He didn't stay there long. When the doorbell rang, he jumped up and ran to the door barking ferociously.

"Horatio, it's only Harley. Go lie down," Quinn commanded. "Everything's fine." She opened the door and her heart stopped beating for a moment as she looked up at Harley, who was wearing a black ribbed sweater and jeans and looked so attractive, she felt her knees go weak. How would she ever manage to keep him at a distance when he had this violent effect on her?

"Good evening, Quinn." He leaned over and gave her a quick kiss, then held out a small bouquet of flowers he had concealed behind his back.

"Harley, you don't need to bring flowers every time we meet," Quinn protested.

"Just say thanks and enjoy them, Quinn," Harley answered, smiling.

"Thanks." Quinn forced herself to return his smile, while turning and walking into the kitchen to find a vase. Harley followed her and as she reached up into the cupboard to take the vase down from the highest shelf, she felt his arms slip around her and hold her close to him.

"Let me help you." He nuzzled her and kissed the back of her neck.

"You have a funny way of helping. I almost dropped this, you startled me so." She turned around to face him.

"I've been dreaming of you all week and wanting to hold you like this." He took the vase and flowers out of her hands and put them on the counter. Then he gathered her in his arms and held her close. "Mmm, you smell good. Is that a new perfume?"

"Dani made me buy it." Quinn grimaced. "She's a real tyrant."

"I applaud her taste. It's perfect on you." He nibbled

her ear then left a trail of kisses along her jawline, till he reached her mouth. Then he kissed her deeply.

Quinn gathered all her strength and pushed him away. "Aren't we supposed to be at the restaurant at seven? It's almost that now," she asked abruptly, feeling her heart racing and her knees go weak.

"You're so hardhearted, Quinn. I don't suppose Theo will give away our table if we're not there right on time." He kissed her again and Quinn could feel herself begin to give in to the emotion sweeping through her. Then, with seeming reluctance, Harley pulled back. "I guess you're right. We'd better go, or I won't be held responsible for my actions."

Quinn picked up her jacket from the sofa in the living room and Harley helped her into it. They headed toward the door, stopping to say good-bye to Horatio on the way. With a last glance back Quinn closed the door, locking it behind her.

They drove to the Apollo in silence, both lost in their own private thoughts. Harley had a CD playing, a slow dreamy classical piece. As Quinn listened to it, she debated the wisdom of her decision to end the engagement. One side of her, the rational side, knew it was time to get out of the situation before she got hurt. The other, the romantic side, didn't care about the cold, hard facts. It wanted to give in completely to her heart. She groaned out loud without realizing it. From past experience, she already knew which side would win.

"What's wrong, Quinn? Are you feeling all right?" Harley looked concerned, his brow wrinkling.

"I'm fine." She looked for a handy excuse. "I just

remembered I forgot to feed Horatio. He's going to be hungry by the time I get home."

"Don't worry about him. Isn't he a little overweight anyway?" Harley asked casually.

"Honestly, Harley, don't you ever give up?" Quinn lashed out quickly at Harley, who recoiled in surprise from her sharp tone of voice. "You've always got something negative to say about Horatio. I can't understand it. What did he ever do to you?"

"Sorry," Harley backtracked quickly, seemingly realizing he was on thin ice. "Let's call a truce on Horatio. I promised to give him a chance and I will. Let's just enjoy our evening."

From that moment on, Harley was the perfect host. He had asked Theo to reserve the same table they'd sat at the first time they dined together. There was a bottle of champagne on ice beside it when they arrived, and he had ordered their meal in advance, so Theo brought their appetizers right away. They settled into their dinner like a longtime couple.

A strolling musician came over to the table and although Quinn was embarrassed, Harley gave him some money to play for them. The first piece he played had a light upbeat tempo that made them smile. The second was a slow, sad love song that Theo translated for them, telling them about a fisherman who went to sea and never returned. Every evening, his beloved waited for him on the shore.

Quinn felt tears come to her eyes and she excused herself hastily to go to the powder room and repair her makeup. What had gotten into her? She didn't know why she felt so sad. Oh, who was she trying to kid? Of course she knew. She could see herself in that story. The woman waits for her beloved; the man never returns. That was what would happen to her when Harley left, which inevitably he would.

She knew in that moment she just couldn't go through with putting an end to the engagement. She would take Dani's advice. No regrets, and no more talk of calling things off. She would stay with Harley until *he* decided it was over. She'd deal with the heartache when it happened, not before.

Quinn ran a comb through her hair and applied a little more lipstick, then looked in the mirror again. Her cheeks were flushed and her eyes bright with excitement and vulnerability, like a young girl on her first date.

Harley was waiting when she returned to the table. "I think it's time I took you home, Quinn. Are you ready to go?"

"Yes, it's been a long day. I'm feeling tired."

The drive back to her apartment took only a few minutes. Quinn fiddled nervously with her seat belt and her hair, taking a few strands and twisting them round and round. Finally Harley pulled up in front of her apartment.

"Would you like to come in for a drink?" she asked anxiously, hoping he'd say yes. She was relieved when he nodded and got out of the car, coming around to open the door for her. As she alighted, he put his arm around her and she rested her head on his shoulder.

"I thought you'd never ask. If you think Horatio will let me," he added with a smile.

"I can't speak for Horatio. You'll have to make your own peace with him. But as for me, I think it might be quite nice." She smiled up at him. Luckily it was dark enough that she was sure he wouldn't see the love shining in her eyes.

Once inside the apartment, Quinn went into the kitchen to find two glasses and a bottle of seltzer water. As she came back into the living room, she saw Harley crouched down in front of Horatio, talking earnestly to him. Her heart warmed at the sight of the two of them with their heads together. She stood silently watching for a moment before announcing her return.

"Well, old boy, I guess you and I are going to have to get used to each other. What do you say?" Harley reached out and ruffled Horatio's fur. Horatio responded eagerly by licking Harley's face. Quinn expected Harley to back off, but he didn't. He stroked Horatio gently.

"Why, Harley, you old fraud!" Quinn said. "I believe you really are a dog lover after all."

"I don't mind dogs, as long as they behave themselves." Harley turned toward Quinn with a quirky smile on his lips. "Horatio says it's okay if I kiss you," he added slyly.

"I didn't hear him say that." Quinn laughed, walking toward Harley who had crossed the room to the sofa. He took the glasses from her and set them on the coffee table.

"Come here, Quinn." She sat obediently next to him and he reached up to turn her face toward his. "Let me love you."

I wish you did, Harley, Quinn thought as his face descended toward hers.

Quinn woke up to the insistent ring of the telephone. She reached for the receiver groggily.

"Wake up, Quinn, I'll be over in half an hour for breakfast." Harley had taken a room at the Empress Hotel the night before so he wouldn't have to drive all the way back to Duncan. He had suggested to Quinn that they spend the following day together.

"You will, will you. You're taking your life in your hands. You know I don't cook."

"Even you can't ruin fresh croissants. I'll bring them with me. Put the coffee on."

"Yes, sir." Her heart soared as she anticipated their day together.

Springing out of bed, she walked into the bathroom, turning on the shower. When the water was hot, she hopped in and after a scalding wash and cold rinse, her skin tingled and she glowed with good health. She dressed quickly in a T-shirt and shorts and went into the kitchen to put on the coffee.

She wondered what would it be like to have breakfast with Harley every morning and felt a pang of sadness that it could never happen. But she banished her sad thoughts, deciding to enjoy the day and worry about the future later.

She prepared a tray of orange juice and coffee and carried it into her study, where she put it down on the table she normally used as a desk. The table was situated in front of a bay window that looked out onto the back garden.

The doorbell rang and Horatio, a little slow on the uptake, barked ferociously.

"Hey, Horatio, it's just Harley. You're going to have to get used to him."

She hurried to the door and opened it to see Harley

loaded down with several bags of fresh pastries. He
set everything down and pulled her into his arms.

"Harley, let go." She laughed, struggling against his
grip.

"Not on your life," he said playfully. "What about
a good-morning kiss?"

"What about your breakfast?"

"I want you for breakfast." He began to kiss and
tickle her at the same time, until she giggled help-
lessly. Horatio let out a couple of loud barks, not sure
if his mistress was enjoying herself or needed help.
Then as the couple kissed he grew suspiciously quiet,
as he sniffed the bags of goodies Harley had set on
the floor.

"Horatio!" Quinn broke off the embrace just in time
to see Horatio trying to make off with the bag of croissants. As she spoke sternly he dropped it and slunk
away to his mat, not daring to give her a backward
glance.

"Where was I?" Quinn said as she resumed her lingering kiss with Harley then relaxed against him, enjoying the warmth of his embrace.

"Don't get too comfortable, Quinn. We've got lots
to do today."

"We do? And just what might that be?"

"We're going to have ourselves some fun."

He grabbed the breakfast muffins and pastries he
had so carelessly abandoned a few moments before,
and Quinn led him to the table where they ate their
breakfast while they made plans for the day.

"I think we should go to Chinatown and wander
around, have a look in some of the interesting shops.

Then we'll pick up some food and go to the beach for a picnic. Look at that sun." He glanced out the window into the backyard. "It's going to be a great day."

"What about Horatio?"

"What about him? He can come along, as long as he promises to behave."

"In your Mercedes?" Quinn regarded Harley, disbelief written all over her face.

"Why not? I'll just spread a rug on the backseat so he doesn't tear the leather with his nails, and he'll be fine. I'm sure he'll like it."

"Like it? He'll love it. He loves the wind ruffling his fur. It's the only time he gets a good look at what's going on around him, when the wind blows the hair out of his eyes." Quinn chuckled at the thought of Horatio sitting in the back of Harley's Mercedes, the wind blowing his ears and his fur straight out behind him.

She fed him quickly and cleaned up the breakfast dishes. Then they gathered up the things they would need for the picnic and set off.

Chinatown was alive with activity even though it was Sunday. They parked and walked through the huge ornate gates marking the entrance to the small city within a city. The grocery stores were already bustling with shoppers and the colorful displays of fresh fruits and vegetables looked enticing. Though Quinn didn't recognize many of the exotic vegetables, she found the fruits inviting and bought mangoes, bananas, and grapes for the picnic, along with pork buns and some sweets.

In a shop that sold wicker ware, Harley spotted a

picnic basket complete with a set of dishes and utensils
and insisted on buying it. They loaded all their food
purchases into the basket, then stopped at a convenience store for cold soft drinks before setting off in
the car. They had left Horatio in the Mercedes while
they explored the alleys and shops of Chinatown and
when they arrived back at the car he greeted them
enthusiastically, bestowing kisses on both. Harley put
the top down on the car and rearranged Horatio's rug,
telling him to lie down. He obeyed immediately. He
must have known he needed to be on his best behavior, Quinn marveled.

"Don't worry, you'll get a nice long walk on the
beach today, Horatio. It won't be long," she promised
him. She settled into her seat.

"Ready, Quinn?" Harley checked to see if she had
put on her seat belt.

"Yes, sir." She saluted. "Let's go!"

They drove along the coast of the island, toward the
town of Sooke and then past it to French Beach Pro-
vincial Park. Although there were a few cars in the
parking lot, Quinn was relieved to see it wasn't
crowded. She hopped out and pulled the seat forward
to let Horatio free. After he danced around a little,
barking excitedly, she called him over and snapped on
his leash. Harley took the picnic basket out of the
trunk of the car.

"All set? Let's find a table and we'll leave the basket there while we give Horatio a run. Then we'll eat.
I'm starving already. After lunch we'll take a longer
walk."

"Sounds perfect." Quinn grabbed the straw hat she
had thought to toss in the backseat when they'd left

her apartment. Squashed and misshapen, it looked as though Horatio had sat on it. "How does this look?" she asked, balancing it on her head.

Harley laughed. "Like one of those wicker platters we saw in Chinatown."

Quinn took the hat and punched and pushed it back into shape, then plunked it back on her head. "I'm ready."

They dropped the picnic basket off at a table not far from the beach, then took Horatio down near the water and let him off the leash, so he could run. He ran toward the water, then stopped and sniffed it, backing up quickly as the waves lapped at his feet. He was like a young puppy, playing tag with the waves as they rolled in. Quinn laughed delightedly at his antics.

"What a clown!" She spoke to Harley, thinking he was standing next to her. He wasn't. She had been so engrossed in watching Horatio that she didn't notice Harley had disappeared. Puzzled, she turned and looked back in the direction from where they had come, spotting him a short distance away. He had stopped and was engaged in earnest conversation with a petite blond. The woman was immaculately dressed in a cute little sundress that revealed more than it concealed. She was carrying her sandals, which had high heels and tiny leather straps the color of her dress. She looked gorgeous, but totally out of place among the families of sunbathers and picnickers.

Who was this woman and why was she looking so possessively at Harley? Quinn felt a wave of jealousy descend upon her like a storm cloud as she watched Harley's dark head bend toward the woman's blond

one. The blond had her hand on his arm and was cling-
ing to him for dear life.

Quinn couldn't bear to watch anymore. She called
to Horatio and took off at a run down the beach, leaving Harley far behind. When she had rounded a bend
so she was no longer visible to him and his blonde
friend, she headed for the nearest log, then sat down,
out of breath. Horatio, who was panting hard, plopped
down next to her, seemingly glad of a rest.

Why did she feel so angry? Harley was not her private property. He was forty-five and had certainly
lived life fully before she met him. Why did it hurt so
much to see him talking to another woman? Quinn
knew the answer. She was jealous because she loved
Harley but was unsure of the depth of his feelings
toward her. She wanted their relationship to be for
real, not a hoax. She wanted him to love her as she
did him. Seeing him talking to a beautiful woman was
a cruel reminder of the fact that sooner or later he
would get tired of playing the little game he'd concocted, and when he did, he'd be gone out of her life
forever. Try as she might she just couldn't change that
reality.

To add insult to injury, this tiny, attractive woman
reminded her of her own feelings of clumsiness and
inadequacy growing up a giant next to a dainty mother
and sister. She felt big, awkward, and ugly. It took all
her strength to keep from bawling but she refused to
give in to her feelings in public.

She spotted Harley marching down the beach toward her and she pulled herself together, feeling her
heart harden. Horatio went running enthusiastically to

meet Harley, racing back and forth between Quinn and him until Harley reached Quinn.

"Why did you run off like that, Quinn?" Harley seemed genuinely puzzled. He seemed to have no idea why she was upset.

"I thought perhaps you wanted to be alone with your *friend*." In spite of trying to remain cool and aloof, Quinn spat out the word angrily as though it were poison.

"Don't tell me you're jealous of Sandra?" He laughed easily. "Remember I told you I'd been involved with someone and was glad of our agreement because it gave me an excuse to break it off? It's been over between us ever since that night you and I first had dinner together."

"Nevertheless, I can see how our little bargain is cramping your style, Harley. I think it's time we called it off," Quinn said stubbornly before she had time to think through the consequences. "After all, it's gone far beyond what either of us envisioned or wanted. I, for one, would like to be free to date other men," she insisted, though it was a big, fat lie.

Harley looked surprised. "If that's what you want, I won't try to stop you," he replied tersely. He turned away from her, a scowl on his face. "Too bad; I thought we had something special going for us."

"What's so special about a phony engagement? It's just a lot of lies. The deal was that either of us could call off the arrangement anytime, and I want out now. Please take me home." She turned and started walking back up the beach to where the picnic basket was still sitting on the table, a cruel reminder of the fun day they had planned.

Harley followed in a moment, finally catching up with her at the picnic site. "At least, let's eat lunch before we leave. I'm hungry."

They ate in stony silence, gathering up the dishes and carrying the basket back to the car. Quinn tried to brush the sand off Horatio before he jumped up on the car seat, but it was impossible. He made sandy paw prints on the rug and seat. Harley glared at them both.

The ride home was spent in icy silence, with Quinn gazing out the window, close to tears, and Harley staring straight head, not even glancing in her direction. Quinn couldn't stop thinking how foolish she'd been to become jealous just because Harley had been talking to another woman. But she was too stubborn to apologize and try to put things right. She'd pay dearly for her impulsive behavior.

When they reached the apartment, she got out of the car and let Horatio out of the backseat. As she closed the door, she tried to say good-bye to Harley but the words got stuck in her throat.

"Are you sure this is what you want, Quinn?" Harley asked, giving her a last chance to change her mind.

"I'm sure," she insisted, feeling all the while that her nose was going to start growing like Pinnochio's if she told one more lie.

Harley sped away without another word. *What have I done?* Quinn thought, berating herself as she stood alone on the sidewalk. The enormity of her actions began to sink in. It no longer seemed enough that she had Horatio to keep her company. She dreaded going into her apartment where signs of her and Harley's breakfast together would be evident.

She opened the door and headed straight for the bedroom where she cried herself to sleep.

Chapter Nine

When Quinn woke up, the room had darkened and although she had no idea what time it was, she knew she'd been asleep for some time. She glanced at her clock radio and saw it was already past 8:00. Getting up reluctantly, she went into the hallway where she noticed the light blinking on the answering machine. For a moment her spirits rose as she thought perhaps it had been Harley who'd called. Then she realized he had no reason to—she was the one who had called off the engagement, not he. Her spirits plunged again just as quickly as they had risen. She pushed the button and listened to the message.

"It's me, Dani. Is everything okay? I need to talk to you about the thirteenth. Call when you get home."

Oh, no, the book-signing! Quinn suddenly remembered Harley's promise to arrange Herbert Davis's appearance at the store. She wondered if he'd call it off.

I have to call and find out if it's still on, she thought, dreading the idea. Before she could lose her courage she quickly dialed his number.

"Yes?" Harley's husky voice sounded even more masculine than usual, if that was possible, a cruel reminder of all that Quinn had lost.

"Harley, this is Quinn," she stuttered.

"Yes?" His voice became cold and clipped.

"I'm sorry to bother you," she faltered, wondering how to ask him about Herbert Davis. "Dani was calling me about arrangements for the thirteenth and I just wondered—"

"You needn't have worried," he interrupted her, his voice steely. "I have no intention of going back on my word. I said Davis would be there and he will. Is that all you wanted?"

"Well, there is the matter of the engagement ring. I don't want to trust it to the mail or a courier. If you don't mind, I'll return it to you the next time I come to visit my parents."

"Hang onto it for now. I'll pick it up when I come to Victoria for the book-signing."

"Oh, so you're planning to come with Davis?" Quinn felt unreasonably happy that she would have an opportunity to see Harley again, then her spirits plummeted as she realized how painful that would be.

"Of course. Now if there's nothing else, I'll say good-bye. I've had a rather trying day."

Quinn hesitated. "Harley, I'm sorry."

"Don't be," he said abruptly. "You were absolutely right. Things got out of hand. Better to call it off now than to let it get even more complicated. I'll see you on the thirteenth." He hung up abruptly without saying good-bye.

After she hung up, Quinn wanted to climb right back into bed and pull the covers up over her head, but she forced herself to return Dani's call.

"Dani, it's me."

"Where have you been, out with your fiancé?" Dani teased.

"We did go out earlier, but I've been home for a while. I was asleep when you called."

"Asleep? Are you feeling all right? You're not sick, are you?" Concern could be heard in Dani's voice.

"No, I'm fine." Quinn hesitated. "Well, actually I'm not fine at all. I feel horrible. Can you come over?"

Dani didn't even hesitate. "I'll be right there."

Quinn tidied the apartment while she waited for Dani, trying to erase all signs of Harley from her life. She washed the dishes and put them away, then regretfully took off the engagement ring and tucked it away in her dresser drawer for safekeeping. She was about to throw out the beautiful flowers Harley had brought the night before when the doorbell rang and Dani walked in.

"Quinn, shouldn't this door be locked?"

"Oh, I forgot, I guess. Come on in. Would you like some tea or coffee? I was just going to make something for myself."

"Tea, please. I'll never sleep if I have coffee this late at night. Now, tell me, Quinn, what's going on? You look awful. You've been crying," Dani accused. "Your eyes are all swollen."

Wordlessly Quinn held out her left hand, minus the ring. "It's over," she said in a monotone.

"What happened? I thought things were going so well."

"They were, but as usual, I messed up. Why am I so hopeless?" The tears threatened to start flowing again, but Quinn immediately jumped up and busied herself with the kettle and teapot, and by the time the tea was ready she had regained control.

Explaining what had happened earlier in the day, she finished, "So it's over. Logically I know it was only a business arrangement anyway, but it was starting to feel so real. We were having so much fun."

"Why don't you just call and apologize?" Dani questioned.

"If you could have heard his voice when I called a while ago, you wouldn't even suggest that. I had to check with him about the book-signing after I got your message," she explained. "I suddenly realized he might not be willing to go through with it. But he said he would," she quickly reassured Dani, who looked startled.

"Thank goodness. We've spent good money on the caterer and advertising, not to mention all the hard work. That would be an even bigger disaster. Now, I say don't worry about this little lovers' spat with Harley. Perhaps it was time for your crazy agreement to end anyway. Now that it's over, Harley will come to realize just how important you are to him and he'll soon be back. And this time, no bargains. It'll be for real. Just you wait and see," Dani tried to reassure Quinn.

"I don't think so, Dani." Quinn started to feel a tiny ray of hope, but then she remembered how angry Harley had been. "And just when he was starting to get on so well with Horatio," she lamented.

"You two were meant for each other. Trust me. It's going to work out. Now, I don't want you sitting by the phone, waiting for him to call. We've got to keep you busy, so if he calls you won't be home. You can start by baby-sitting for me tomorrow night. My fella and I would like to go out without the kids for a change. What do you say?"

Quinn agreed. The two women chatted amicably over tea and by the time Dani left, Quinn was feeling much better. She didn't have Dani's optimism about Harley but she knew life would go on, and she had no choice but to get over him and go on with it.

The next few days sped by as Quinn and Dani made final arrangements for the thirteenth. Both of them put in long hours and Quinn was often at the store long after it closed. On Friday night, the week before the book signing, after having put in an especially long day, Quinn decided to stop at the Apollo for dinner rather than worry about preparing something to eat when she got home.

She called Theo and asked him to prepare her usual meal, saying she'd be there in half an hour. She used the time to go over her list of tasks once more, ticking off the ones that were completed and starring the ones she would tackle the next day. Just before she estimated her dinner would be ready, she walked the short distance to the restaurant. She wondered if it was a good idea to go to the Apollo considering the last two times she'd been there had been with Harley, but then she decided she wasn't going to give up her favorite restaurant just because the memories might hurt. She resolved to enjoy her meal and opened the door decisively.

Theo came out from behind the counter to greet her. After asking about Horatio and about Dani and the store, he led her to her table. Quinn noted that he was headed straight for the table where she and Harley had sat on the two occasions they had dined together. She asked if he didn't have another table he could give her, but then she noticed that there were RESERVED signs on most of the other tables, all except a couple of the bigger ones that were used for large groups of people. She shrugged and followed him meekly.

She had barely got settled and taken a sip of her wine, when she spotted Theo coming toward her again, empty-handed. There was someone trailing behind him but until he was almost in front of her, she couldn't see who it was. Then as they drew closer, she realized it was none other than Harley.

"Forgive me, Quinn, I am very busy tonight." Theo pointed toward the reserved tables. "I must ask you to share your table with Mr. Donaldson. I know you are friends, so I think you don't mind, right?" Theo beamed at them, and Quinn, for all her misgivings, couldn't help but smile. He thought he was doing them both a favor, playing matchmaker with his two favorite customers.

"I don't mind if Mr. Donaldson doesn't." She looked up at Harley, holding her breath and waiting for his reaction.

"Thank you, Theo. Ms. O'Connell and I would be happy to share a table." He sat down and Theo rushed off to fetch him some wine.

"Good evening, Quinn." He regarded her with a serious look and Quinn tried to decide if he was pleased to see her or if he would rather have dined alone. His expression gave nothing away.

"This is quite a surprise. I wasn't expecting to see you," Quinn replied.

"Why not? You know I often come here when I'm in Victoria."

"Yes, that's right, you did mention it," Quinn said quickly.

"I must admit, though, I hadn't thought to see you either. I thought you'd be too busy preparing for the book-signing to be dining out."

"Perhaps if you had been expecting to see me, you would have chosen another restaurant tonight," Quinn gave voice to her thoughts.

"Now why would you say that? I know we parted on unpleasant terms the other day but, after all, we're both adults," Harley said smoothly. "We should be able to see each other occasionally without making a big deal of it. After all, you'll be visiting your folks from time to time. We were bound to run into each other sooner or later."

"Yes, of course," Quinn replied quickly, wishing she could be as nonchalant as he, but knowing her face was much more transparent and would give her away.

"And how is Horatio?" Harley asked.

"Why do you ask?" Quinn asked defensively. "I know you don't like him so it's rather insincere, don't you think? Or are you afraid he's lurking under the table, getting ready to jump out and steal your roast lamb? I assume you are having the lamb, as usual?"

Quinn was all sarcasm, even though she herself had ordered the same deep-fried squid she always had.

"How did you ever reach that conclusion about Horatio?" Harley asked coolly. "I think he's actually quite a nice mutt. Anyway, I know I'm safe here. Theo wouldn't want to run afoul of the local health inspector, so I know if Horatio were anywhere, he wouldn't be inside the restaurant. I repeat, how is he?"

"Harley Donaldson, you told me you didn't like sheepdogs," challenged Quinn. She had forgotten how infuriating Harley could be.

"I don't think I ever said that outright. I may have said I preferred short-haired breeds, but I don't recall saying I didn't like sheepdogs."

"Well, that's certainly the impression you gave. I don't know what to make of you sometimes."

"I could say the same thing of you. I still don't understand why you were so upset the other day at the beach. We were enjoying ourselves until you got it into your head to have a temper tantrum. What ever possessed you to get all upset just because I was talking to Sandra? She has nothing whatever to do with you and me." Harley sat back and took a sip of his wine, waiting for Quinn's response.

"Perhaps not." Quinn could feel herself beginning to heat up. Harley could be so obnoxious, acting so superior at times. She couldn't tell him she'd been jealous because he had been so engrossed in Sandra, and it had made her realize how tenuous their relationship was and how much she cared for him. "Seeing you with Sandra made me realize that our agreement was cramping your style," Quinn equivocated. No way she would admit her jealousy.

"Don't you think I should have been the one to decide that? Maybe I liked our agreement, as you call it. I prefer to call it an engagement," Harley replied smoothly.

"Call it whatever you want. It doesn't change the fact that it's over. Things have worked out for the best, I'm sure you'll agree."

"I certainly don't agree. I was quite happy with the way things were going, and I thought you were too. After all, our goal was to get our families to stop pushing marriage on us. We certainly accomplished that."

"Yes, but—"

"Look," Harley interrupted, "before we find ourselves angry with each other again, let's just enjoy our dinner. Here comes Theo with our meal."

"You're right, there's no point in going over and over the same territory. It's too late to do anything about it now."

"Do you think so? There's nothing to stop us from picking up where we left off . . ." Harley suggested casually.

"No way!" Quinn insisted. The thought of returning to her arrangement with Harley scared Quinn silly. Unless he was willing to enter into a real relationship, she had no intention of torturing herself again.

At that moment, Theo arrived at the table with Quinn's salad and deep-fried squid, and Harley's roast lamb. He smiled and winked at Quinn, then as he walked back toward the kitchen she noticed him pick up some of the RESERVED signs off the tables closest to hers and Harley's and carry them back to the desk. Of all the—! She wondered if Harley had put him up to that little stunt, or had he thought it up on his own?

It couldn't have been Harley. He hadn't known she
would be coming to the Apollo tonight. It must have
been all Theo's idea. What a hopeless romantic.

Quinn and Harley put aside their differences long
enough to enjoy their meal. The only other disagree-
ment they had was when the check arrived. Harley
insisted on paying and, try as she might, Quinn
couldn't get him to change his mind. Then he offered
to walk her to her car. She agreed reluctantly, it being
late and dark out and she being parked a few blocks
away, near the store.

When they reached the car, Horatio was waiting for
her. He had been asleep on the back seat and jumped
up, barking as they approached.

After greeting Horatio, Harley turned to Quinn.
"Quinn, will you go out with me tomorrow evening?
I'm staying in town for the weekend," Harley ex-
plained.

"I don't think that's a good idea," Quinn replied,
though she was dying to say yes.

"Why not?" Harley insisted.

"You said once that I wasn't attracted to you, nor
you to me. Let's just leave it at that."

"You're lying to me and to yourself, and I'll prove
it." Harley pulled Quinn toward him, against his broad
chest. His head came toward hers. Quinn tried to break
away, but he held her tightly. Try as she might, she
could not avoid his lips, which met hers. For a moment
she tried to resist, but as he kissed her, she felt herself
succumb. Finally she broke away from him.

"Harley, don't! Leave me alone."

"Oh, I'll leave you alone all right. Just don't try to

tell me that you don't feel anything." He smiled cruelly. "It's not over between us yet, Quinn, just wait and see."

"Oh yes it is. I don't ever want to see you again," Quinn blurted out.

"Is that so? What about next Friday night?"

Quinn started to stammer a reply, realizing he was talking about the event at the store, but Harley cut her off.

"I thought so. You don't mind if I bring Herbert Davis to the store next Friday, but otherwise you don't want anything to do with me. I should have known what kind of woman you were." He turned and walked away disgustedly, leaving Quinn to watch his back disappear into the darkness.

Quinn got into her car and drove toward home. She couldn't believe Harley thought she would use him just to get Herbert Davis to the store. He must have a pretty low opinion of her. If only she could tell him the real reason she didn't want to see him: she was in love with him and could not risk him finding out.

Over the next few days, Quinn and Dani continued preparing for the book-signing, even though Quinn wasn't sure Harley would show up with Herbert Davis. She didn't think he would be cruel enough to call it off at this late date but she hadn't heard from him since the previous Friday. She decided to behave as if the event would go ahead as planned, hoping he was the man of honor she thought him to be.

At last the thirteenth arrived and, after working on last-minute details, Quinn and Dani closed the store early to set up the tables and to allow themselves time to go home and change. The signing was scheduled to start at seven. Dani put up the decorations and called the caterers one last time to make sure they knew to bring the appetizers just before 7:00. She and Quinn had purchased sodas, filling a huge bin with ice to keep the sodas cold. The caterer delivered glasses and they polished them to shine away any spots, then set them out on the linen-covered table. There were candles placed strategically around the store. The setting was perfect for a visit from the undisputed champion of romance.

Just before it was time to reopen the doors, Quinn dashed home to change and drop off Horatio. With so many people coming, he'd be better off at the apartment.

She showered quickly and put on the last new outfit remaining from her shopping spree with Dani. It consisted of a creamy silk tunic over black form-fitting slacks. The slacks emphasized her long slim legs while the top accentuated her tan. Her hair had grown out a little from the short cut she normally sported and was slightly wavy and shiny. She wore a beautiful amber-and-silver pendant and earrings her parents had given her for her thirtieth birthday. The amber picked up the highlights in her hair, and the effect was stunning. She hoped Mr. Herbert Davis would appreciate her efforts.

As Quinn drove up to the bookstore, she was surprised to see a line had formed in front and was snaking its way down the sidewalk, already halfway to the corner. It looked as though half the women in Victoria, and a few men, had come to meet Herbert Davis and have him autograph his new book.

Quinn felt her spirits lift. Then she spotted Harley's Mercedes pulling up across the street. Her stomach did a flip-flop. Thank goodness he had arrived, but why was he alone? She parked her car and walked quickly to the store entrance, tapping lightly on the glass. Dani opened the door a crack and she slipped in.

"Did you see all the people?" Dani clapped her hands in glee. "Everything's ready. It's nearly seven; I wonder where Davis is?"

"I just saw Harley parking across the street but he was alone. There was no sign of Herbert Davis. He must be coming in his own vehicle. Oh, what if he doesn't show up?" Quinn was worried, but in actuality it was more about how she and Harley would manage not to argue and bicker during the book-signing, rather than whether Herbert Davis would show. Harley had promised the writer would be there and in spite of their differences, she knew he wouldn't let her down.

"Don't worry, he'll be here and everything will work out just fine." Dani was reassuring herself as much as Quinn.

"As for Harley, I almost wish he hadn't come. I don't want to see him. What if I get upset or start bawling? You know how I feel," Quinn worried. Dani knew only too well. In the days since Harley and Quinn had terminated their engagement, Quinn had cried on Dani's shoulder more than a few times.

"For heaven's sake, Quinn, it's going to be all right. Now, pull yourself together. There's Harley at the door. Go and open it." She gave Quinn a slight push from behind and Quinn stumbled forward, then regained her balance and went to unlock the door.

"Hello, Quinn."

Harley seemed perfectly calm and composed, not like Quinn, whose hand shook as she remembered their last run-in. He looked so handsome and serious, Quinn felt as though her heart would break.

"Hello, Harley," she said, trying to appear cool and collected. She figured the only way to get through the evening was to act as though she didn't care two hoots about him.

"Everything ready?"

"Yes, come in and I'll show how we've got things set up." She led him to the table where Herbert Davis would be seated and showed him the stacks of books ready to be signed. "Would you like a glass of water?"

"Thanks. The store looks good. You've done a great job." He glanced around and spotted Dani near the buffet table. "You must be Dani." He walked toward her, his hand outstretched. "I'm very pleased to meet you. Quinn's told me all about you."

He smiled his most dazzling smile, dimples and all, and Quinn's spirits plummeted. He had found an ally in Dani, who appeared captivated.

"Not half as much as she's told me about you, I'm sure," Dani joked.

"Dani," Quinn protested, then turned away to cover her embarrassment. "It's almost seven, are you sure Herbert is coming, Harley?"

There was a strained silence. Harley looked at Quinn guiltily. Then he looked around him, hesitating as if he were the bearer of bad news.

"Quinn, I have something to tell you."

"Oh no, don't tell me he can't make it." Quinn's heart sank and her grip on the bottle tightened.

That was all she needed to make her life a total disaster.

"No, no, it's nothing like that," Harley quickly reassured her.

"Then can't it wait, Harley?" said Quinn impatiently. "I'm too nervous right now to worry about anything other than getting this event under way. We can talk later, when the evening's over. Look at all the people out there. We're going to have to open the doors soon with or without Herbert."

"What I have to say can't be put off another minute," Harley insisted urgently. "Come here." He grabbed her hand and led her toward a quiet corner of the store, away from the door and Dani's curious eyes and ears.

"Haven't you been even mildly curious as to how I was able to guarantee Davis's presence here tonight?"

"I just thought he was your friend," Quinn stammered.

"Didn't you notice that my initials are H. D., the same as his, and wonder about the coincidence?"

Quinn gave him a puzzled look. What *was* he getting at? Truthfully, she hadn't even noticed their initials were the same.

"Have you taken a good look at the picture on the back cover of the Davis book recently? I mean, since we've gotten better acquainted?"

Quinn stood there mutely, not understanding what Harley was getting at. She picked up one of the books and turned it over, examining the picture on the back. All of a sudden, a light came on, and she realized what he was hinting at.

"You? You mean to tell me *you're* Herbert Davis?

I don't believe it." Her skepticism showed on her face. She studied the picture once again as if to eliminate any possibility of Harley and Herbert being the same person.

"Believe it, Quinn."

"But what do *you* know about romance?" she stammered nonsensically. "There's no one in the world less romantic than you. How could you have written all those wonderful books?"

"Well," Harley drawled, "I've never had any complaints in the romance department, that is, until I met you."

"Of all the—" She stopped in mid-sentence. "No wonder you looked so familiar when we met." Quinn started to see red. "You lied to me, you fraud."

"Now just a darned minute," Harley interrupted before she could launch into a tirade. "I didn't lie to you. I've never lied to you about anything. Think back to our previous conversations and you'll realize the subject just never came up. It didn't seem to occur to you that I might be Davis and I never volunteered the information, but I didn't lie. At worst, perhaps I'm guilty of being a little evasive, but certainly not a liar. Not many people know about my second career, only a few close friends and family. The only reason I'm letting you in on my little secret is because I'm trying to help out a woman I just happen to be in love with. So don't go getting all self-righteous on me. Now open the doors and let's get this circus under way. We can talk later and I'll explain everything. My public awaits." Harley took a pen out of his pocket and sat down at the table next to a stack of his books, waiting expectantly for Dani to open the door and let in the hordes of women who were clamoring at the door.

Quinn was so taken aback to learn that Harley was, in fact, Herbert—or was Herbert really Harley?—that she totally ignored what Harley had just said. She had a million questions running through her head, and no time to ask them as Dani opened the door and let in the first wave of women. *You're darned right you'll explain everything later, Mr. Harley Donaldson, or whatever your name is!*

The store became a mass of confusion and Quinn was forced to station herself behind the counter to ring in sales and assist people in finding the books they requested. Dani stood guard at the door, letting more people in as others left. It was pandemonium for over three hours.

In the meantime, Herbert Davis chatted calmly with adoring women as they sipped wine and ate the appetizers and tiny sandwiches supplied by the caterer. Dani made coffee and delivered one to Herbie, as the ladies were affectionately calling him. He was so busy signing books and talking to his appreciative fans that he couldn't get away from the table. The event was supposed to end at 10:00 but it was closer to 11:00 when the last customer finally left the store and the door was locked. The evening had been a huge success with all the books sold and many more ordered.

Quinn's thoughts were in a jumble, just like the store. In an effort to keep busy and avoid Harley, she tidied the counter, wishing it were as easy to sort out the confusion in her head. As she went around the store picking up empty glasses and plates, she avoided looking at Harley who was drinking coffee and talking earnestly to Dani. How could she face him after this? She felt like such a fool. She wondered idly what he and Dani could be discussing but chose to continue cleaning up rather than find out. Finally Dani got up and came over.

"Boss, I'm going home. I can't stand on my feet another minute. And you should do the same. I propose we come in early tomorrow morning and finish cleaning before we open. The worst is done and we're both too tired to do any more now. What do you say?" she asked.

"What?" Quinn asked absently. "Oh, yeah, that's a good idea. Thanks for all your help, Dani. You were wonderful." Quinn hugged her helper and walked with her to the door.

"Now, Quinn," Dani whispered, "be nice to the man, he's done you a great service. Do you have any idea how much he values his privacy? I think you should say thank you and apologize profusely for your behavior at the beach the other day. From what you've told me, you didn't have any reason to be so angry."

"I will certainly thank him, but I don't know about the apology. I'll have to see. Now get going home and I'll see you in the morning. Is eight o'clock all right with you?"

"No problem. Eight o'clock it is."

As Quinn turned to walk back into the store, she saw Harley watching her intently. She became totally self-conscious. That man—he had a real knack for making her feel flustered. Knowing she had to approach him sooner or later, she walked slowly to where he was sitting.

"Harley, I want to thank you for everything you've

done for me and for the store," she started awkwardly.
"It must have been hard for you to give up your privacy for all this notoriety. Now you won't even be
able to walk down the streets of Victoria without being
recognized. You were a smash hit. How did you come
to start writing romances?" Quinn knew she was bab-
bling, but she couldn't seem to stop.

"It's a long story, but to make it as brief as possible,
as part of my work, I used to read and write a lot of
dry, boring manuals for computer software. I started
writing romance as a way of relaxing. I didn't really
intend to sell my stories. Once, when I was sending
one of my manuals off to the publisher, a couple of
chapters of a romance novel I was working on accidentally got clipped onto the back of the manuscript.
When the publisher read them, he passed them on to
a friend who specialized in publishing romance fiction.
I quickly found out there was more money to be made
in the romance field than in writing technical manuals.
These books have given me a very nice income. I decided to use a pseudonym for the romances since they
were such a departure from the work I was known for.
And maybe I was a little embarrassed about them too,"
Harley admitted. "After all, there aren't many men
writing in the genre. That's why I cultivated a reputation for being a recluse. I didn't want to have to do
public appearances and blow my cover."

"Then I'm doubly appreciative of what you've done
for me." Quinn busied herself picking up the rest of
the empty cups and glasses and fussing around the
snack table. "It's been a long night and you must be
tired." She tried not to notice that Harley had got up

from where he had been sitting and was rapidly approaching. She wanted to run and hide.

"Quinn, we have to talk about us," Harley said quietly.

"No, Harley, not tonight. I'm too tired to deal with any more stress. I need to go home to bed. Eight o'clock will come awfully early tomorrow morning. Are you driving back to Duncan tonight?"

"No, I've taken a room at the Empress. I'll go home tomorrow. I had hoped we'd be able to spend some time together and try to sort things out."

"I don't think that's wise, do you?" Quinn countered. "We got ourselves in quite a mess before with our little bargain. I have yet to explain to my parents that we're not getting married. I just can't cope with anything else at the moment. Let's give ourselves a little time, then perhaps we can be friends," she finished weakly, knowing she sounded like an idiot, but not daring to say what was in her heart.

"I don't want to be your friend, darn it. Don't you understand? You are the most stubborn, infuriating woman I've ever met." With that Harley stormed out of the store, calling over his shoulder, "When you're ready to talk sensibly, give me a call." The door slammed behind him.

Chapter Ten

T he silence in the store was deafening after Harley's abrupt departure. The crowds and confusion of the evening had kept Quinn's mind occupied until this moment; now she had no choice but to think about Harley. She poured herself a coffee and sat down, looking around her.

All her hopes and dreams of the past three years were contained in this store. But strangely, it didn't seem enough anymore. Before Harley, a career, her friends, and Horatio had been all she wanted. Now she realized she needed a loving relationship with some-one, a man like Harley who was intelligent and kind, fun to be with, and a hunk. Why was it that every time they got together they fought? It had been a stormy few weeks yet when he wasn't around her life seemed empty and meaningless.

Quinn pulled herself up out of the chair and prepared to go home. Realizing she had a lot of money in the cash register, she emptied it into a plastic bag and put it in the large satchel she used as a purse. She would take it home with her until she could get to the bank in the morning. It would be a real tragedy if, after all their hard work, there was nothing to show for it. A few establishments in the downtown area had been burglarized in the past few months. She flipped on the security system as she let herself out the door, walking the short distance to her car. Then she drove to her apartment.

Horatio was waiting by the door and she could hear him dancing and yelping as she struggled with her key. Why had she forgotten to leave the porch light on when she had gone out earlier? She let herself in and walked quickly to the back door to let him out for a run.

The apartment seemed emptier than usual, and she felt alone and sad. She had a fleeting thought that she'd like to call Harley at the Empress Hotel, but dismissed it quickly. No, as much as she wanted to see him, she needed time alone to think things through. Was there a future for them? What had he said tonight, something she had wanted to remember later and reflect on? No, it was gone. Too much confusion, too many people. She needed a good night's sleep. Horatio yelped at the door, this time from outside, and she let him in.

As Quinn was getting changed in the bathroom, she thought she heard a noise in the living room, but she didn't pay much attention. She wasn't worried, as she knew Horatio would bark at an intruder. Too keyed up to sleep, she put on a sweatsuit and carried her clothes into the bedroom to put them away. She thought perhaps if she read for a while it would help her relax.

As she stretched out, Quinn noticed that her apartment, which had always seemed just the right size, now felt too large and empty for her liking. It seemed to need another person to fill it. What had Harley done to her?

She heard a tiny whimper from the other room and thought it strange that Horatio hadn't come into the bedroom as he usually did. Perhaps he had gotten himself stuck behind the couch. She got up once again and went into the living room. There was no sign of Horatio. Quinn switched on the light and started as she realized she was not alone.

"If I were you I'd be quite concerned about security in this apartment. Do you realize I had no problem at all getting in? Even Horatio, who's supposed to be your loyal watchdog, didn't seem to mind. He didn't even bark." Harley was standing in the middle of the living room, his arms folded across his chest.

"Harley. You startled me," Quinn stammered. "How did you get in?"

"The door was unlocked. You must have forgotten to bolt it."

"Horatio," Quinn called, looking around for the dog and wondering why he hadn't barked at Harley.

"Don't worry about him. He's in the kitchen chewing on a bone. He's very easily bribed." Harley smiled wickedly.

"What are you doing here? What do you want?" What was Harley up to? Quinn was puzzled.

"I came to see you."

"I thought I told you I didn't want to talk tonight."

"You may not want to talk to me but I want to talk to you. Get your jacket. You're coming with me."

"Harley—" Quinn protested.

"Never mind arguing." Harley brushed Quinn's objections away impatiently. "It's too late for that. Let's go." He went into the kitchen, took Horatio's leash off the hook beside the door and snapped it on his collar. "Come on boy, let's go." Horatio trotted obediently after Harley. Quinn had no choice but to follow them out to the Mercedes, which was parked in front of the house.

"Get into the car," Harley ordered. "We're going for a ride."

"Harley, it's late," Quinn tried to insist, but Harley interrupted her again.

"That's why there's no sense in arguing. Just come with me. I just want to get you away from here so we can talk without interruption."

Realizing it was useless to argue, especially with Horatio sitting in the back of the Mercedes as large as life, Quinn got into the car. She closed the door, deciding stubbornly not to say anything to Harley. He might want to talk but that didn't mean she had to. She'd show him she didn't appreciate his strong-arm tactics.

She needn't have worried about talking. Harley drove silently, not once looking at her. She wondered where he was taking her, but didn't want to give him the satisfaction of asking. They headed out Douglas Street, following it until it became the Island Highway. They seemed to be heading in the direction of Duncan. Perhaps he was taking her to his place. At least from there she'd be able to escape and go next door to her parents' house.

But Quinn should have known that wasn't what Harley had in mind. When they reached the summit of the Malahat Highway, he pulled off the road, turning into a hotel called the Sea View Resort, a luxury accommodation high on a bluff overlooking the ocean. Quinn had passed dozens of times without stopping. Telling her to wait, he went into the lobby and came out a few moments later with a key dangling from his hand.

"That's our cabin over there." He pointed to a small cottage away from the main lodge. "They don't allow dogs in the main building," he offered by way of explanation.

He drove to the cabin and parked in front, taking a bag out of the backseat next to Horatio and letting him jump out. Quinn got out and closed the door. She looked around. It was dark, after midnight, so she couldn't see the view, but from the location, guessed that it would be spectacular.

Harley unlocked the door to the cabin and stood aside for Quinn to enter. She stepped through the doorway and looked around. It was a beautiful log building with a small stone fireplace against one wall. There was a living room with an eating area and a tiny alcove of a kitchen. The bedroom was off to the left. Had circumstances been different she would have been enchanted by its quaintness.

"Harley, this is ridiculous. I have to be at work early tomorrow. I told Dani I would be at the store at eight o'clock." Quinn's nerves were jumping as she tried to figure out what Harley wanted.

"Well, I told her otherwise. I arranged for a cleaning company to go into the store and clean up, under Dani's supervision. She knows you won't be around for the weekend. You and I need to spend some time together and see if we can't sort things out."

"You mean to tell me Dani knew about your plan? I'll kill her." Quinn paced angrily up and down the cottage.

"Don't be mad at her. It's not her fault. I swore her to secrecy. Come and sit down beside me."

Reluctantly, Quinn went over to the sofa and sat down. She turned away from Harley, feeling betrayed by Dani, yet curious as to why Harley felt it so important to spend time with her especially since their bargain was off and their last meeting had been such a disaster.

"Quinn, I've never had to 'kidnap' any woman before. Usually any woman I'm with is more than willing to be in my company. But you and I seem to have got off to a bad start. I couldn't think of any other way for us to get some time alone. You seem determined to spurn me. I admit it's partially my fault. I should never have suggested that crazy arrangement of pretending to be engaged. It just muddied the waters. But then I didn't know I was going to fall in love."

"What?" Quinn looked up, startled.

"I'm in love with you. Haven't you figured that out yet? Do you have any feelings for me, or were you just playing a part when we kissed?"

"Do you think I'm the kind of woman who could kiss someone without having strong feelings for them? If you do, then I don't know why you're even interested in me." Quinn turned away from him. He put his hand gently on her arm.

"Let's not fight. I hoped by coming here this weekend, we might start over, get to know each other. Let's forget what's gone before and see if we can build a new relationship, based on honesty and trust."

"I don't know." Quinn considered his words but was not convinced. "I feel as though you've kept too many secrets from me. How can I trust you now?"

"We're starting over, remember? Things are going to be different this time. What do you say? Are you willing to give it a try?"

"I'm not sure." She thought for a moment and then, impulsively, in true Quinn fashion, made up her mind. "All right, we'll try. But can we start in the morning? All I want to do now is go to bed. I'm exhausted and it's very late."

"Agreed. You can sleep in the bedroom and I'll sleep on the couch." Harley patted the couch as if to test for comfort. "I think it makes into a bed."

He reached out and pulled her into his arms. His dark head descended and his lips met hers, ever so lightly. "Good night, Quinn, sweet dreams. Oh, by the way, this bag has some of your things in it. Dani packed it for you." He handed her the bag that had been on the back seat of the car.

Quinn undressed and climbed into bed. What a strange turn of events! She couldn't believe she was lying in bed in a little cabin, perched at the summit of the Malahat Highway, with Harley sleeping on the couch in the next room. After their fight earlier in the evening, she'd thought she'd never be this close to him again. When she got over feeling angry, she knew she'd think it was kind of romantic. He'd swept her away just like the hero in *The Happy Captive*. She felt the tension of the day drain out of her as she drifted off to sleep, a smile on her lips.

"Quinn, wake up!"

"What? What's the matter?" Quinn opened her eyes and for a moment, forgot where she was. Then she saw Harley standing at the end of the bed, holding a tray. "What's that?" she asked sleepily.

"Breakfast. And you'd better get up right now, or it will be cold. Come and sit in the living room."

"I'll be right there." She got out of bed quickly and ducked into the bathroom to brush her hair and teeth.

"Have you been up long?"

"No, I ordered breakfast for nine o'clock, and woke up when I heard room service knocking on the door. Would you like some coffee?"

"Please. I hope it's good and strong. Dani has spoiled me for regular coffee. She makes it so strong the spoon stands up in it."

"It looks and smells great. Here, come and help yourself."

Quinn served herself a plate of fresh fruit, croissants, and jam, then sat down at the small table near the window. Harley opened the curtain, and Quinn gasped in pleasure.

"Look at that view! Oh, Harley, what a beautiful spot."

"I thought you'd like it. After breakfast we'll take the car and drive down to the park near the water. Then Horatio can have a nice run on the beach. He got cheated the other day."

"Don't remind me; I thought we were starting over," Quinn said ruefully.

"We are. Forget I said that," Harley said quickly. "How are you feeling?"

"I feel great. That's the first good night's sleep I've had in ages."

"Funny, I haven't had much sleep either these past couple of weeks," Harley admitted. "Now what would you like to do today?"

"It's been so long since I've had a Saturday off that I hardly know what to say. Let's see." Quinn thought for a moment, then said, "I know, let's drive to Chemainus and have a look at the murals. I haven't stopped there in ages." Chemainus was a small town north of Duncan whose main attraction was the colorful murals painted on the outside of buildings around the town. The murals depicted the area's history. There were also many interesting little shops, some catering to people interested in antiques and collectibles, something Quinn loved.

"Do you know, I've never stopped in Chemainus?" Harley said. "Usually when I am traveling that stretch of road, I'm in a hurry to get to Victoria or going home and trying to beat the traffic. That's a great idea. I asked the kitchen to pack us a picnic lunch so we can stop when we feel like it and we won't have to worry about Horatio."

"Oh, Horatio." Quinn looked over guiltily, remembering that she didn't have any food for him. "What can I give him to eat this morning?"

"Don't worry, I brought along some dog food and a dish. I'll put something out for him. Then we can take him for a little walk before we set out. Why don't you have your shower while I take care of him?"

"Thanks, Harley." Quinn looked at Harley shyly. "You know, this wasn't such a bad idea of yours. I think I'm going to enjoy myself."

Harley got up and came around to where Quinn was seated. She stood up to meet him, gazing into his eyes.

"Me too." He took her in his arms and kissed her soundly. "Good morning, Quinn." He gave her a hug and then let go of her. "Going slow with you is the hardest thing I've ever done. You are so beautiful, I don't ever want to let you out of my arms." He gave her a little push toward the bathroom. "Away you go, before I change my mind."

For the first time in as long as she could remember, Quinn sang in the shower. She felt on top of the world. When she and Harley could manage to get along, it felt wonderful. She hoped it would never end.

The day passed quickly and they had a marvelous time. Harley enjoyed the murals, Quinn the antique shops, and Horatio the beach and picnic. All too soon, they were back at the hotel, preparing for dinner.

"I've made a reservation for seven, Quinn. Can you be ready by then?"

"No problem. I'll just have a quick shower and get dressed, then it's your turn. I wonder what Dani packed for me to wear?"

"I told her to put in that little red number you had on the other night. You look stunning in it. Did I mention you're a very beautiful woman, Quinn?"

"I think you may have, but I don't mind hearing it again. All my life I've felt big and clumsy and not very cute, next to my mother and sister. It was hell being so tall when I was growing up."

"Well, whatever you went through was worth it, because I can't resist you. You're just the right height for me."

"What do you mean?" Quinn asked, loving his compliments and wanting more.

"Come here and I'll show you." Quinn walked over to where Harley was standing.

He reached out and drew her toward him. His head came down and he kissed her long and hard. "You see, just the right height."

Quinn, wanting the kiss to go on forever, reached up to touch his lips.

"Oh, no you don't, you vixen. We'll never make our reservation if you do that." He reached over and gave her a swat. "To the shower."

"Yes, sir. I won't be long."

By 7:00 they were both dressed and ready to go over to the restaurant in the main building. Harley said he'd heard the menu was superb, and they weren't disappointed. The decor was casual but elegant. There were fresh flowers and candles everywhere.

They looked at the menu and found a diverse selection of dishes. Quinn decided on poached salmon, served with a Hollandaise sauce, and Harley ordered the prime rib of beef. They were both starving after their busy day and dug into their meals with enthusiasm.

"I've asked the chef to give me a doggy bag for Horatio."

"Harley, I really appreciate the effort you're making with him. I know you're not really a dog lover."

"Actually, I have one final confession to make." Harley looked sheepish and Quinn wondered what was coming.

"Oh, no." She groaned. "What is it this time?" She didn't want anything to ruin the magic of the evening.

"About dogs. Remember the picture on the back of my book? The one of me sitting in a garden with a big Old English sheepdog?"

"That's right!" Quinn exclaimed. "I had completely forgotten. Harley, you're a man of many contradictions," she teased.

"When I was married to Felicity, we had a wonderful Old English sheepdog named Bruno. It was he in the picture. He died in the accident along with Felicity. I've never wanted to become attached to another dog since. It was so hard losing my wife and our dog at the same time. When I was grieving for my wife, it seemed silly to even mention Bruno. But it was like everything important had been taken from me at the same time."

"Oh, Harley, I can't even imagine how you must have felt; I'm so attached to Horatio. No wonder you were leery of getting to know him. But Harley, you can't avoid caring for people or dogs just because you might lose them someday."

"I'm beginning to understand that, Quinn. And it's you and Horatio who have taught me. Have you finished your coffee? Come on, let's go back to our room."

They walked arm in arm to the cottage. Horatio was overjoyed to see them. They let him out to run. While they admired the clean, fresh air and the millions of stars twinkling in the heavens, he found an area behind the cottage, which had been left natural with long grass and huge cedars and firs. He wandered around for a few minutes, then came running back.

"Are you ready to go in now, Quinn or do you feel like going out somewhere?"

"You know what I'd like? Do you think we could light a fire in that fireplace and relax in front of it? That would be the perfect ending to our day."

"Sure, I'll light the fire while you go back over to the restaurant and order us some more coffee."

Quinn walked quickly back to the hotel. She ordered coffee and drinks and while she was waiting, decided to use the pay phone in the lobby to call Dani. She wanted to let her know that everything had worked out fine and to make sure things had gone well at the store that day. She quickly dialed her number hoping to catch her at home. Dani answered after two rings.

"Dani? It's Quinn. You've got a lot of explaining to do," she joked.

"Quinn, I'm so glad you called. I didn't know how to get hold of you. Harley didn't tell me where he was taking you, only that you'd be gone for the weekend." Dani sounded upset.

"What's the matter? Is there a problem at the store?"

"Tell me you took the bank deposit home on Friday night. When I came in on Saturday there was no money in the safe."

"Oh, Dani, I hope you haven't been too worried. I did take it home. It's still there."

"Good; that's one problem resolved. There's something else I have to tell you." She hesitated.

"What is it, Dani?"

"It's about your father. Your mother called the store looking for you today. Your dad's had another heart attack. He's in the hospital."

"Oh, no! When did it happen?" Quinn felt as though she'd been punched in the stomach. She leaned against the wall for support, her legs like jelly.

"Late last night. He was brought to Victoria from Duncan by ambulance. He's in the Victoria General Hospital. Your mother's there with him."

"Can you call the hospital and get a message to her for me? Tell her I'll be there as soon as I can."

"I'll go over there myself and tell her," Dani offered.

"Thanks, Dani. I'll see you later."

Quinn canceled the coffee order and raced back to the cabin. The tears started to flow as she took in what Dani had said. It was as if she'd wandered into a bad dream and would wake up in a moment and everything would be all right. She burst through the cabin door where Harley was about to light the fire.

"Harley, quick, I just talked to Dani," she said frantically. "My father's had a heart attack and he's in the hospital in Victoria. I have to go right away." She rushed into his arms and he held her closely.

"Calm down, Quinn. If your father's in the hospital, he's getting the best of care. I'll pack our things. You get Horatio and put him in the car."

They both raced around getting ready to leave and within ten minutes were on their way to Victoria. Quinn was thankful she was with Harley as she knew she would not have been able to drive, as upset as she was. She prayed her father was all right and that nothing would happen before she could get to him.

Since they weren't far from Victoria, in less than an hour they were pulling up in front of the hospital.

"Oh, Harley, I'm so afraid. What if he's not okay?"

"Let's not jump to conclusions, Quinn. We don't know how serious it is. He may be just fine. Come on and we'll find out where he is." Harley helped Quinn out of the car and put his arm around her shoulders as they walked toward the hospital door.

They walked quickly to the reception area and asked where they could find Howard O'Connell. The receptionist asked if they were family. Harley took over.

"This is Mr. O'Connell's daughter and I am her fiancé."

The receptionist checked her computer. "Ms. O'Connell, your father is in the intensive care unit. I'll show you how to get there." She walked into the corridor with them and pointed to the elevators. "Just take this elevator to the fourth floor and when you get off, turn right. He's in room 413."

Quinn paced up and down the hallway as she waited for the elevator. When it finally came, they got in and rode to the fourth floor without speaking. As they alighted, Quinn spotted her mother sitting in a waiting area down the hall.

"Mother, how's dad?" Quinn embraced her mother.

"Oh, Quinn, I'm so glad you're here. I haven't been able to reach Carol and Jeff. They went away for the weekend. The doctor says these next forty-eight hours are critical but if he makes it through them, he'll have

a good chance of complete recovery. I'm so worried."
She broke down, and Quinn held her close.

"It's okay." Quinn patted her mother's back. "Harley and I are here now. Will the nurses let me see him?"

"They only allow one person at a time, and only family."

"Why don't you go in, Quinn, and I'll sit with your mother. Marjorie, come and sit down. Now, tell me, have you had anything to eat today?" Harley talked to Mrs. O'Connell while Quinn slipped into the room to see her father.

He was hooked up to every sort of machine imaginable, it seemed to Quinn. He looked old and fragile lying there surrounded by tubes and wires. A nurse was sitting in the corner, monitoring his condition.

"How is he?" Quinn asked.

"He's holding his own. He's been drifting in and out of consciousness so he may not recognize you. Don't be alarmed. It's just the drugs he's been given to allow him to rest comfortably. You can approach the bed."

Quinn tiptoed forward and stood beside her father. His eyelids flickered and Quinn could tell, by the way his eyes lit up briefly, that he had seen her.

"Dad, what's the big idea? What have you done? Don't worry, the doctor says you're going to be fine. You need to stay quiet though and get lots of rest. Don't fret about mother. Harley and I will take care of her. I'll be sitting right outside in the hall if you need me." She went back outside, tears forming. She brushed them aside, not wanting her mother to see how worried she was.

"Quinn, your mother hasn't eaten all day. Why don't I take her down to the cafeteria while you stay here with your father?"

"That's a good idea. Mother, you have to keep up your strength. If there's any change, I'll send someone to find you, I promise."

Harley took Mrs. O'Connell's arm and led her to the elevator. Quinn sat back in the chair, prepared for a long wait. She wasn't going to leave the hospital until she knew her father was recovering.

The vigil at her father's bedside continued for two days. Harley was a godsend, taking first Mrs. O'Connell and then Quinn for meals or for a walk around the grounds of the hospital to get some fresh air. He insisted they get some sleep and took one, then the other back to Quinn's apartment for a few hours each night. There was always someone at the hospital in case they were needed. He even delivered Horatio to Dani's, so she could look after him until things returned to normal.

Finally, on the Tuesday after the heart attack, the doctors declared Mr. O'Connell to be out of danger. They moved him to a room on the ward and the family was able to breathe a little easier. Harley had made himself very useful both to Quinn and her mother, and to Dani at the store. He filled in ably for Quinn in her absence, staying in town at a friend's rather than driving back and forth to Duncan.

Within a couple of weeks, Mr. McConnell's doctor decided he was well enough to go home to recuperate.

On the day he was released, Harley volunteered to drive him and Louise back to Duncan.

"Are you sure I don't need to go along?" Quinn asked her mother as Harley came by the apartment to pick her up for the trip to the hospital and then to Duncan.

"No, Quinn, Harley will make sure we get home safely, won't you Harley?"

"I sure will. Don't worry, Quinn. Why don't you go down to the store and see if Dani needs a hand? She's been putting in a lot of extra hours while you've been at the hospital."

"You're right. If I'm not needed, I have lots to do here. I'll be up on Saturday night, Mother. Say hi to Dad for me. And thanks again, Harley. I don't know what we would have done without out your help."

Quinn watched them drive off and she thought about what Harley had done for them. Now that life was getting back to normal, she would have to think of a way to repay him.

Chapter Eleven

During her father's illness and subsequent recovery, Quinn and Harley had not managed to spend a single moment alone. With her mother staying at the apartment and Harley staying with friends, they had nowhere to go to be alone. Harley's carefully planned weekend at the Sea View Resort had ended abruptly when Quinn's father had suffered the heart attack. Quinn made up her mind that the two of them should find a way to finish what they started.

Quinn had acknowledged to herself a long time ago that she loved Harley but she had never told him. That weekend at the Sea View, he had told her he loved her but she hadn't had a chance to reciprocate. Since her father had gone home, life had been busy. She had been putting in long hours at the store and she didn't know what Harley was doing but he hadn't been to

Victoria. They hadn't even spoken on the phone all week.

It was difficult with the two of them living in different cities. It seemed to Quinn that their romance had reached a standstill. She was afraid his silence meant he was no longer interested in pursuing their relationship. Quinn made plans to visit her parents, and while she was in Duncan, she would pay Harley a visit.

The week seemed to drag but finally Saturday arrived and Quinn was more than happy to get away for the weekend. She and Horatio set out for Duncan as soon as she locked the doors. Traffic was light and the trip pleasant, allowing Quinn time to unwind before arriving. She was anxious to see her father. Even though she talked to her mother regularly, she wanted to see for herself how his recovery was progressing.

As she pulled into her parents' driveway, she noticed there were no lights on at Harley's and the Mercedes was not in the driveway. Her spirits sagged. She had hoped he'd be home so that they could spend some time together.

"Mother, Dad, where is everyone?" Quinn called out as she opened the kitchen door.

"We're in the living room. Come on through."

Quinn left Horatio in the kitchen and went into the living room. Her father was sitting in his easy chair beside the fireplace and her mother sat opposite him, knitting and watching television.

"Dad, how are you feeling?"

"A little stronger every day, Quinn. I feel better than I've felt in a long time. Your mother and I have been going out for walks every afternoon. The doctor says it's good for me to get a little exercise."

"That's great. How about it, Mother, has he been behaving himself?"

"He's been just fine," Marjorie confirmed.

"Have you seen much of Harley lately?" Quinn hoped her tone of voice was casual enough to disguise her worry from her mother.

"No, we haven't. When your father first came home from the hospital he popped over every day, but now that life is getting back to normal, he hasn't been around much. He may be out of town at the moment. I haven't seen his car for a few days. He didn't mention anything before he left. Haven't you spoken to him?"

"No, mother, I haven't. I've been so busy at the store," Quinn explained. "I tried to call a couple of times, but he wasn't home."

"I hope everything's all right between you two?" Her mother looked up questioningly. "Why, Quinn, I just noticed you're not wearing your engagement ring. Is there anything wrong?"

Quinn didn't know what to say. She didn't want to tell her mother and father that the engagement was off, when it might be on again for real. Why get them upset for no reason? She decided to stall for time.

"You're right. I took it off when I was cleaning and forgot to put it back on. Well, I'm going to have a shower and fix myself a sandwich." She quickly changed the subject. "How about I make us all a nice cup of tea?"

"That would be lovely, dear," her mother said.

Later as Quinn got ready for bed, she couldn't help

feeling disappointed that Harley wasn't home. Although she had wanted to visit her parents, one of her main reasons for coming to Duncan for the weekend had been to spend time with him. Perhaps he would come home before she left the next evening. She vowed to make the most of her visit in any case, promising Horatio an early walk on the beach.

In the morning, Quinn awoke at her usual time. She was up and in the kitchen, making coffee at 7:00. Horatio paced up and down the kitchen. He seemed to know they would be going for a walk as soon as Quinn finished breakfast. She ate a bowl of cereal and drank some orange juice, then grabbed a jacket and Horatio's leash and off they went.

They started down the trail toward the water, Quinn walking at a relaxed pace and Horatio running in front of her. He was overjoyed to be loose and ran ahead, then back again, checking to see where she was. He always did many more miles than she, doubling back constantly. She lost sight of him as he rounded a bend in the trail, but she knew he wouldn't wander far.

A loud bark up ahead alerted her to the fact that someone else was on the trail. She began to wonder if it was just a squirrel or raccoon Horatio had discovered when he didn't come running back to her. Watching the ground so she didn't trip or twist her ankle on a tree root, she began to jog, so she could catch up to him. She ran round the bend and right into a solid object.

"Ouch!" Quinn gasped as she bounced back, momentarily dazed. She had been moving at quite a clip and hadn't noticed someone advancing toward her. Now she saw it was her one-time fiancé.

"Harley!" Quinn's face lit up with pleasure. "It's so good to see you." She reached up to give him a kiss, but he turned his face away.

"Hello, Quinn," he said coolly.

What was wrong with him? He was behaving so strangely.

"It's nice to see you, Harley," she said tentatively. "Have you been away? I didn't see your car when I arrived last night."

"I got in quite late. I caught the last ferry over from Vancouver. I had some business to attend to. I've been away a lot lately."

Was it Quinn's imagination, or did Harley seem evasive and distant?

"Is everything okay?"

"Fine."

"I'm sorry our weekend at the Sea View Resort was spoiled. We'll have to try again sometime," Quinn ventured.

"I don't know if that's such a good idea."

"Oh? You seemed pretty keen at the time," Quinn insisted, feeling frantic. What was wrong with him?

"Well, since then I've had some time to think things through. And I've come to the conclusion you were right when you said we should cool things. Maybe one day we can be friends as you suggested."

"Why the change of heart?" Quinn asked, her mind reeling. She had just begun to believe him when he had said he loved her.

"I've given our relationship a lot of thought and I've decided I'm not ready for commitment. It wouldn't be fair to continue seeing you when I don't know if I'll ever be ready. You see, I don't ever want to lose someone I love again. It's too painful. I just can't go through what I went through with Felicity. When I saw your father in the hospital, it brought back some very painful memories, ones I'm not ready to deal with."

Quinn started to do a slow burn. "I think I'm finally beginning to understand you, Harley Donaldson." She could hear her voice getting louder. It was as though she was standing outside her body, watching the two of them from a distance. "You're just a big chicken, that's what you are. Did that phony agreement you concocted have anything to do with these feelings of yours? Were you using it to disguise your fear of involvement? You can't avoid loss, you know. Sooner or later it happens to all of us."

"Not if we don't let ourselves fall in love. Not if we just keep everything casual and lighthearted. I'm sorry to disappoint you, Quinn, but I think it's best that we don't see each other again for a while." Harley turned and started back down the path toward the beach.

"Disappointment, is that what you think I feel?" Quinn couldn't believe Harley, but she realized there was no sense in arguing with him. "If that's what you want, there's nothing I can do about it, but I think you should know I love you, Harley Donaldson," Quinn called out to his retreating back. "I've loved you almost from the first night we met. And I thought you loved me. You're right about one thing though. We'd better not see each other again because I won't be satisfied with a casual affair or an on-again, off-again romance. If I can't have you completely, I don't want any part of you.

"You see, my father's heart attack has made *me*

realize I want to get married and have children soon while my parents are still around to spoil them. Too bad; I thought you felt the same way I do," Quinn finished, out of breath. The shock of Harley's about-face had sent her into a tailspin. Her chest heaved with emotion. She knew he had heard her, though he kept on walking.

Quinn called to Horatio and started running up the trail toward her parents' house, trying to put as much distance between herself and Harley as she could. She knew she was going to burst into tears and once she started she didn't know if she'd be able to stop.

"Quinn, I'm sorry," Harley called out, and this time it was her turn to keep on walking.

The rest of the weekend was a nightmare. Quinn put on a brave front for her parents, not even mentioning she had seen Harley. As soon as she could get away, she went back to Victoria. Being next door to Harley and not being able to see him was more than she could bear.

With a heavy heart she contemplated her future and realized she didn't like what she saw. Before she met Harley she thought her life was full. Then he came along and swept her off her feet. Now he was gone, and she realized just how much she had been missing. How could she go back to an empty life when all she wanted was him?

When Quinn went to the store on Monday, Dani could tell from her pained expression that the weekend had not gone well. Quinn told her what had happened, and Dani was sympathetic at first, but after a while

she got tired of hearing Quinn whine about how unhappy she was. Finally she confronted her.

"What are you going to do about it?" she finally
asked, after watching Quinn mope about the store,
hardly speaking or smiling.

"What do you mean? What can *I* do about it? Harley
doesn't love me and he doesn't want to be with me."

"Wrong on both counts," Dani countered, her dark
eyes flashing and her face determined. "Didn't Harley
tell you he loved you?"

"Yes, but . . ."

"And didn't he seem to enjoy being with you?"

"I think so, but . . ."

"Never mind the buts. He loves you and he wants
to be with you. From what you told me of your conversation, he didn't say his feelings had changed. But
past experience has taught him that when he loves
someone, he loses her. He's afraid. He doesn't want
to have to go through the pain again. Don't you get
it? You have to convince him to take a chance. Someone as smart as you shouldn't have any problem finding a way to break down his resistance. I didn't think
you were a quitter, Quinn. You surprise me, you really
do. If you really love Harley, you'll fight for him."

"I don't know, Dani." Quinn hesitated, dubious of
Dani's conclusion. "He seemed pretty definite it was
over."

"Of course he did; he had to convince you, didn't
he? But I would have thought you'd be able to see
right through his little ruse. Do I have to tell you
everything, Quinn?"

"No." Quinn thought for a moment. "So all I have
to do is break down his resistance? That shouldn't be

so difficult. I can be as stubborn as he is, right?" Quinn brightened up and began to smile.

"Right, you're the queen of stubborn." Dani smiled, relieved the gloomy look was gone from her friend's face.

"Will you help me, Dani?"

"You bet."

It took Quinn a day or two to come up with a scheme to win Harley back, but when she did, she was convinced it was the most brilliant bit of work she'd ever done. When she told Dani her plan, Dani got a real kick out of it.

"Quinn, there's hope for you yet. I wondered if you'd ever get up the courage to go after what you want. Finally you're developing a little spunk. Now, what can I do to help?"

"You can do what you did for Harley when he spirited me away for the weekend; take over the shop while I'm gone. If all goes according to plan, you won't see me for at least a week."

"I can handle it. Even the mighty Quinn is not indispensable." Dani laughed.

Quinn busied herself making arrangements for her little surprise. She called a travel agent and booked a flight for two. She made a reservation for Horatio to stay at a kennel. She packed a suitcase for herself and one for Harley, going out and buying the few articles of clothing she thought he would need. A call to her parents confirmed that all was well. She told them she wouldn't be coming to Duncan that weekend.

"Don't say anything to Harley, if you happen to see him. I'm planning a little surprise."

"Why Quinn, this isn't like you," her mother said.

"I'm not myself, Mother. I'm in love, and it's doing strange things to me."

"I'm very happy for you, dear. I'm sure Harley will be pleased with whatever you have up your sleeve. You two go and have a good time."

"Thanks, Mother. Give Dad my love."

Finally Quinn made the most difficult call of all. She called Harley. When he answered she crossed her fingers and started her plan in motion.

"Harley, this is Quinn. I was wondering if you could meet me in Victoria tomorrow? I have something important to discuss with you."

"Oh, what's that?" He sounded offhand, but Quinn was sure he must be wondering what she had on her mind.

"I can't talk over the phone, but I need your advice about a situation that's come up here. You did say we could remain friends, and I really need a friend at the moment. Can you meet me tomorrow at noon, at the Apollo?"

"I'll be there. Is everything all right?" he asked.

"Not exactly, that's why we need to talk. See you tomorrow." Quinn hung up quickly before Harley could ask any more questions.

When she got off the phone she laughed out loud. Harley Donaldson was going to get what he had coming to him. She could hardly wait until noon the next day.

Quinn was very nervous. Could she pull off her plan without tipping her hand? She had never been a good actor, but she needed to be convincing enough to make Harley good and angry.

She dressed carefully for their rendezvous, putting on the sundress he liked so much. Opening her dresser drawer, she took out the engagement ring and dropped it into her purse. Then she drove to the Apollo, arriving about fifteen minutes before Harley was expected.

Theo was waiting for Quinn. She had enlisted his help with her scheme.

"All set, Theo?"

"Yes, Quinn. Are you sure you want to go through with this?"

"Very sure, Theo. This situation calls for drastic action." He smiled and winked, always ready to participate in any game that would further the cause of star-crossed lovers.

Quinn had arranged with Theo for lunch to be ready when Harley arrived. The wine was open at the table and the appetizers were sitting on the sideboard, waiting for Harley to show up. Quinn sat next to the window, watching for his Mercedes. When she saw it pull up and park, she signalled to Theo, and he warned the cook. Everything was ready.

Harley walked into the Apollo right at noon, looked over and saw Quinn sitting at their usual table. His face was drawn and serious. Her heart stood still.

"Harley, thanks for coming on short notice. I really need someone to talk to." She feigned a worried expression.

"You've got me wondering what could be so important that you wanted me to rush down from Duncan in the middle of the day. Aren't you working today?"

"No, I took the day off." Quinn didn't want to be

drawn into a conversation before lunch so she quickly changed the subject. "Let's eat first, then we'll talk. I ordered for both of us, and this time it's my treat."

Theo brought the appetizers to the table. They both tucked into their lunch hardly talking until they had finished eating and were sitting back with their coffee. Finally Quinn judged the right moment had arrived.

"Harley, I want to thank you again for all your help during the recent crisis with my father. I don't know how mother and I would have coped without you."

"I'm glad I was able to be of service. Your parents are very special people."

"I also want to thank you for that evening at the Sea View Resort. I'm sorry it didn't work out as you planned. But I'm glad you introduced me to the place," she said casually. "As a matter of fact, I'm planning to go back there later today. That's what I wanted to talk to you about." She reached into her purse and took out the engagement ring. "Here, I must return this to you. Since we're not engaged anymore, I don't have any right to it. I must say I enjoyed wearing it, in spite of all the problems we had." She put the ring on the table in front of him.

Quinn smiled at Harley, trying to figure out what he was thinking and feeling. The usual cool mask hid his emotions.

"Remember I told you about the fellow I was seeing before you and I made our pact? Well, he has asked me to marry him. I'm meeting my fiancé at the Sea View Resort later this afternoon to celebrate our engagement." Quinn's fingers were crossed under the table, just like she used to do when she was a kid and told a white lie.

Harley's mask slipped at last. He looked totally shocked. At first his expression held hurt, but as Quinn watched, it turned to anger.

"Congratulations!" he said scathingly. "But this is a little sudden, isn't it?"

"Perhaps," she said casually. "However, I took what you said the other day to heart. Since there's no hope for us to be anything more than friends, I have decided to accept his proposal. The poor man has been asking me regularly for years," Quinn added. "You know how it is," she said in an offhand way. "The old biological clock is ticking away. As I mentioned to you the last time we talked, I want to have children and I can't afford to wait much longer."

Quinn could see that Harley struggling to maintain control. He stood up abruptly. "Excuse me if I don't linger over coffee. I must be getting back to Duncan. Thanks for this." He picked up the ring and put it in his pocket. "Good-bye and good luck. I hope you'll be very happy."

He turned and walked quickly through the restaurant to the door, leaving without even a backward glance at Quinn who was still sitting at the table, smiling sweetly. Under the table, her fingers were still crossed and double-crossed. She prayed her scheme would work.

She looked out the window and saw that Theo had kept his part of the bargain. Harley's Mercedes had a flat tire. As soon as Harley arrived at the Mercedes, noticed the flat tire, and opened the trunk to take out the jack, she quickly got up from the table and walked through the restaurant kitchen to the back door, slipping out without being seen. The flat tire on Harley's car would give her time to get to the Sea View Resort before he drove by on his way back to Duncan.

Quinn pulled into the Resort, parking in front of the cottage where she and Harley had stayed on their visit. She walked quickly to the main building to register, then taking the key, went back to the cabin and let herself in. The champagne she had ordered was there in a bucket of ice, along with a tray of snacks on the table. She brought two bags from the car and put them in the bedroom. Then she lit the fire, which had been prepared and was waiting for a match to bring it to life. Now, all she had to do was wait.

Luckily there was a small window facing the front of the hotel and the Malahat Highway. Quinn would be able to see Harley when he drove by. He had no choice but to pass the Sea View in order to get home to to Duncan. She could expect to see him soon. It wouldn't take him long to change the tire, so he couldn't be far behind her.

Quinn sat with her eyes glued to the highway. It was all she could do to sit still, her nerves were in such a state. She didn't have long to wait. Within the half-hour she saw Harley's car come up the hill toward the turn-off to the Resort. She watched, hoping he would do as she had anticipated—spot her car and pull into the resort. He would see her vehicle from the road. She was counting on him looking over at the cabin where they had stayed and being angry enough that he would stop and confront her.

He was slowing down; she saw him look at the

cottage, then at her car. But then, as she watched, holding her breath, he sped up and drove past the entrance to the resort. She hadn't counted on this. And she didn't have a contingency plan. She had hoped if he cared enough, he would be willing to fight for her. He was afraid of making a commitment, especially after losing his wife. He was afraid to let himself love anyone for fear of losing them. That's what she'd counted on. She had hoped his love for her would be strong enough that his fear of losing her to another man would make him act.

Quinn slumped in her chair. She loved Harley with all her heart. She wanted their story to end happily ever after. Tears began to course down her cheeks, and she sniffed loudly. What difference did it make? There was no one to hear or see her. Obviously Harley didn't love her as much as she thought or as much as she loved him.

She got up slowly and went into the bathroom to look for a tissue to dry her eyes. Dampening a face cloth, she wiped her face, wondering what else she could do. There must be some way to get through to Harley.

Suddenly there was a knock on the cabin door. Quinn had left it unlocked for Harley. She heard the doorknob turn and the door open.

"Quinn, are you there?"

She held her breath. It was Harley. Her heart sang with joy. But they weren't out of the woods yet. How would he react?

"Quinn, I know you're in there," he called. "Come out. I want to talk to you."

She gave her face a last swipe with the towel, took

a deep breath, and walked into the living room to face him.

"Harley." She gave him a startled look, her acting worthy of an Academy Award. This was the role of her life. Unless she could convince him that what was he was seeing was real, all would be lost. "What are you doing here?"

"Where is he?" he growled.

"Who?" She feigned ignorance.

"Your fiancé." He walked purposefully toward the bedroom.

"Don't go in there." Quinn's voice was agitated as if she feared a confrontation between Harley and her fiancé. She moved quickly to block the bedroom door.

"Oh, so he's in there, is he? I want to talk to him. He needs to know about us." He paced up and down the small room.

"What's there to know? We had a little fling, but it's over," Quinn said harshly.

"Don't you think he deserves to know you don't love him?"

"Oh, is that all?" Quinn tittered. "He knows, but he loves me and he's willing to take a chance that I'll learn to love him too, over time. You see, Harley, he's not afraid to go after what he wants," she said, issuing a challenge.

"I think he should be told you're in love with me, and I'm in love with you. What chance would your marriage have when you should be marrying me? I can't let you go through with this." He walked toward the bedroom again.

Quinn decided she had made him suffer enough.

"So, you think I should be marrying you?" she confronted Harley, throwing his words back at him.

"Yes, I do."

"Okay, I accept."

"What?" Harley looked confused.

"I accept. You want to marry me. I accept. And, the sooner the better," Quinn added, struggling to keep a straight face.

"But what about your fiancé?" Harley looked totally confused. "How are you going to explain this to him?"

"For someone as smart as you, Harley Donaldson, you say some pretty dumb things. Don't you get it? There is no one else but you. Ever since I met you, you've been the only man for me. When I told you in the restaurant that I was meeting my fiancé at the Sea View, I was talking about you. It's you I want to marry. But I was beginning to think you'd never ask."

"Quinn O'Connell, when I get my hands on you . . ." Harley started toward her. "Of all the dirty tricks!"

"You'll what?" Quinn asked, grinning saucily and standing her ground.

"Come here and I'll show you what," Harley ordered. Quinn walked slowly to Harley, her arms outstretched. He walked straight into them and held her tight, kissing her hair and then her forehead. "Don't ever pull another stunt like that again. I thought I'd lost you for good. We're going to get married right away, so you can't get away from me again."

"I was hoping you'd say that. I just happen to have some airline tickets in my bag. How would you feel about a trip to Hawaii? I just can't go through a big wedding, even to please my mother. My father's not up to it anyway. We can fly to Hawaii tonight and be married there. I have a week off . . ."

Harley silenced Quinn with a kiss. He swept her off her feet, picking her up and carrying her to the sofa. As his mouth came down on hers, he heard her mumbling, "Happily ever after, just like in all the best romances."

GS   4-7-00